Praise for R. Casteel's *Chameleon*

"R. Casteel again carries us away into a world where anything is possible. *Chameleon* is another well-written book whose characters you can't but help fall in love with immediately. This story is a romance of amazing depth, but then one expects that of R Casteel as he weaves a tale of love, intrigue, and personal struggle set in an ultra modern environment. ...*Chameleon* is full of all the best that Science Fiction has to offer, and still maintains its sexy and romantic content for which romance is known. *Chameleon* is a book you will not want to miss."

~ *Romance at Heart Magazine*

Chameleon

R. Casteel

A Samhain Publishing, Ltd. publication.

Samhain Publishing, Ltd.
512 Forest Lake Drive
Warner Robins, GA 31093
www.samhainpublishing.com

Chameleon

Print ISBN: 1-59998-415-6
Digital ISBN: 1-59998-389-3

Editing by Angie James
Cover by Scott Carpenter

First Samhain Publishing, Ltd. electronic publication: January 2007
First Samhain Publishing, Ltd. print publication: April 2007

Chapter One

A dark clad figure, eyes possessed with lust and greed, lurked in the shadows watching the dimly lit window across the road. The time had come. Three years of patience would soon be rewarded with wealth and power.

"You...must finish my work, Khamiel." Her mother made made a feeble attempt to squeeze her hand. "It's all I have to leave you, my dear."

Her eyes slowly closed and a harsh raspy sigh escaped her lips.

Khamiel felt a tear slide down her cheek. She lowered her mother's hand, leaned over and softly kissed her. "Goodbye, Mother." A sob racked her body. "I love you."

Khamiel Roche wrapped her hands around the mug of steaming coffee. The mug, like everything else in the kitchen, was old and chipped. The scarred wooden table bore evidence of long neglect. A block of wood, wedged underneath one leg of the gas stove, kept the relic somewhat level.

She pushed the chair away from the table and stood. It was time to put away her mother's foolish dreams and get back to her life at the FBI forensic lab in Langley. As she opened the pantry door, Khamiel thought back to the countless times she had followed her mother through that door and into the secret world beyond.

The door closed behind her. She released the hidden catch and a panel slid open. Khamiel entered a series of numbers on the keypad and felt a moment of weightlessness. A few moments later, the door opened and she stepped into her mother's ultra modern laboratory.

"Welcome home, Khamiel. Your mother said you would be coming."

The voice came from a speaker located in the ceiling.

"Morning, Max."

"I detect deep sadness in your voice."

"Mother passed away last night." Khamiel ran her fingers over the long black countertop of the lab table.

"I know. Would you like to review the files?"

"No!" she snapped. "I have no time for Mother's foolish dreams."

"Everyone should be so fortunate to be able to follow their dreams."

"What do you know about following dreams?"

"I know she let you follow yours, even though it broke her heart when you chose not to work beside her."

"And end up like her with nothing more than a computer to talk to all day?"

"You are angry."

Khamiel spun around and faced the camera. "Damn right I'm angry," she lashed out. "My mother was one of the most brilliant scientists in the world and she threw it all away...and for what? To live like a rat in a hole chasing a fanatical obsession."

"I remember the hours you spent at my keyboards. Your mind was like a dry sponge and your mother was never too busy to explain something new and help you unlock the mysteries. Your eyes would light up with joy and you would clap your little hands together with such excitement."

"That was a long time ago in another life." Khamiel slowly surveyed the lab. "All this equipment and money could have been used to help others discover new cures and further science."

"Are you so sure it didn't?"

"I *know* my mother." Khamiel slapped the counter with an open hand.

"You know only what you wanted to see. I can open my files and—"

"No!"

"Very well then, Khamiel, delete my files, erase my memory if you must, but before you do, there are a few things you must see. Come into the other lab."

She held her ground refusing to budge.

"Please."

"Oh, all right." She stomped across the floor, flung another door open and stepped inside a large room still painted in Air Force pale blue. Along one wall, plant lights hung suspended over a workbench covered with dozens of pots. At the back of the room, a large steel door closed off the underground tunnel to the elevator in the barn.

She heard the bleating of a sheep, but didn't see the animal.

"Very funny. You play a recording from your files and expect me to..."

Something wet and warm nuzzled her hand and pressed against her leg. Startled, Khamiel looked down to see the head of a sheep turning the same shade of blue as her turquoise slacks.

She jumped back and the animal faded into the background of the straw covered floor. Her legs turned to rubber. Khamiel knelt on the floor and reached blindly to the sides and in front of her. Trembling fingers closed around warm thick wool. Open-mouthed, she gawked in wonder as the sun-darkened hue of her skin spread across the wool.

"Oh! Max!" Tears streamed down her face. "She did it. After all these years, Project Chameleon is a success."

"There is still more testing to be done, but yes, Mother broke the code and was able to duplicate the formula."

"Why didn't she tell me?" Khamiel kept lifting and replacing her hand on the sheep, fascinated with the changing color of the wool.

"That, I do not know, but she was worried the formula might fall into the wrong hands before all the testing was completed."

"Someone approaches the house." A large monitor showed a sports car stop and a tall man with dark brown wavy hair step out.

"That's Agent Haufmyer. We work together..." Khamiel ran for the elevator, "...sort of."

"Do not tell him of this," Max warned.

"Why not? He works for the FBI and I trust him." The elevator door closed and began to move.

The hidden speaker in the elevator crackled. *"For now, follow your mother's wishes...trust no one."*

She stepped from the elevator and, as she closed the pantry door, Leon knocked. Khamiel hurried through the kitchen to the door leading outside, opened it and threw herself into his strong arms. “Leon, what a wonderful surprise.”

“I called the office. They told me you were here.”

“Come in. I’ve missed you. I’m glad you’re here.” She walked back to the table with her arm around Leon. “They didn’t mind you taking time off to come all the way out here to the middle of Georgia?”

He smiled impishly. “I can spare a day. The suits at Langley won’t be the wiser.”

“Leon, your temporary assignment in California has made these last three weeks seem like months.”

California! Alarm bells sounded in the back of her mind. *Damn Max’s warning. I’m going to end up paranoid, just like Mother.*

“I’m sorry about your mother.”

“Thanks. Even though we had drifted apart these last years, losing her like this is a shock.”

“Do they know how she died?” He pulled a chair out, flipped it around and straddled the seat.

She shook her head as she poured Leon a cup of coffee. “Not yet, but knowing Mother like I do, she probably got the flu and decided to treat it herself rather than go to the hospital.”

He leaned his chest against the chair’s back. “Didn’t I read somewhere she was a research scientist?”

She laughed. “You have a good memory.” She set the cup on the table. “Mother hasn’t been featured in any magazines that I know of for years. She hated publicity.”

“Was she still doing research?” He tipped the chair onto the two back legs.

"I…really don't know." She moved away from the table. "We seldom communicated after I went away to school."

He reached for her hand. "What's wrong, Khamiel? You seem edgy for some reason. I thought you might be happy to see me."

"I am, Leon." She glanced at her wristwatch and then at the clock on the wall. "But I have a lot of things on my mind right now and jumping into the sack with you as soon as you walk in the door isn't one of them."

"There's no hurry." He placed all four legs of the chair on the floor. "I plan on sticking around for a couple of days."

"I appreciate the thought, but it's not necessary."

"Wouldn't think of leaving you right now and letting you face this alone."

"In that case…" Khamiel came up behind Leon and put her arms around his neck, "…how can I refuse such a gracious offer?"

He rubbed her arms. "Anything, I can do to help? Contact her friends, associates? Why don't I take her phone book and start making calls?"

"I've already taken care of that," she lied.

"There must be something I can do." He drew lazy circles on her arms with his index finger.

"The funeral home took care of everything." She took a deep breath and caught whiff of a strange exotic perfume.

Ol' hard-cock Haufmyer, you never change.

He stood and stretched. "I think I'll take a quick shower. I've been living in these clothes for days."

"Somehow I find that difficult to believe." Khamiel smirked. "You couldn't go that long without your ration of pussy."

He shrugged his shoulders. "I'm afraid you know me all too well, my dear."

She laughed. "Leon, your cock is legendary among the women in the Bureau, although with regret by some."

"Lies, all lies. Only ones with regret..." he grabbed the front of his pants, "...are those who haven't experienced the greatness of the love king."

"Go take a cold shower." She waved him away. "Only thing bigger around here than your cock is your inflated ego."

Khamiel paced the length of the kitchen. Something wasn't right. She could sense it, but what? She didn't believe his story, not for one second. What was the real reason Leon was here?

Maybe, I should call the Bureau. She reached for the phone.

What if he hears me make the call? Khamiel jerked her hand back, moved away from the phone and went to the kitchen window.

Other than the large old barn with faded red paint and the narrow gravel road, there was nothing but trees. She crossed the width of the house and pushed aside the living room curtain. A large field stretched behind the house and beyond that—more trees.

Mother, why did you have to live so far out in the damn sticks? It was a rhetorical question, because she knew the answer.

One rainy night long ago, an ambulance had brought a car accident victim into the Emergency Room. Most doctors would have given up on the woman's life, but not Marie Roche.

The husband of the woman, an Air Force General on the Joint Chiefs of Staff, showed his gratitude. He'd shuffled paper, cut miles of red tape and handed Marie the deed to a rundown house—in the middle of nowhere.

The house hid the entrance to a missile silo. On paper, the silo had been closed, filled in and forgotten about. In reality, they had locked the entrance and walked away.

Khamiel felt shackled to the house. The result of her mother's work hung like an albatross around her neck. She leaned her forehead against the window and closed her eyes.

"Rough day?" Leon came up behind her, placed his hands on her shoulders and rubbed her sore muscles.

"Mmm. That feels nice."

"I could do a lot better if we went to the bedroom," Leon whispered in a suggestive low voice.

"Nice try." She shrugged off his hands. "But it doesn't feel that good."

"I don't believe this. You're turning down a first-class Haufmyer massage. If word of this gets out, my reputation is ruined."

"Don't worry," she intoned in a dry monotone. "I promise not to tell a soul."

Leon tried to kiss her ear, but she brushed him away. "What part of 'not right now' don't you understand?"

"I'm just trying to help take your mind off things." He trailed his fingers down her arm.

Leon's actions were predictable. He knew all the right buttons to push, but they weren't working this time.

"Things! Damn it, Leon, we're not talking about a table and chair. My mother passed away last night. I might not have been close to her, but she was still my mother."

"I'm sorry, Sugar Bear." He backed away. "I wasn't thinking."

You seldom do. That would require more blood supply to the brain.

"Try it sometime." She forced laughter into her voice. "You might find the experience a refreshing challenge."

She turned around to find him wearing a towel tied loosely around his waist.

"You know something, Agent Roche? There are times when you can be a sarcastic bitch. I came here out of concerned friendship, but I'm wondering now why I bothered."

She walked into the kitchen and stood with her arms crossed under her breasts. "If you feel that way about it, maybe you should put your clothes on and leave."

"Yeah, maybe I should." He yanked the towel from around his waist and tossed it to her. "Thanks for the shower."

Leon stomped down the hall. Several minutes later, he returned partially dressed, carrying his shoes and buttoning his shirt. "You're a real piece of work, Khamiel. You deserve this place. Have a nice lonely, recluse life."

The screen door shut with a *bang*, followed by his car door.

She walked over to the window and watched him leave.

Chapter Two

As Leon drove away, the dust from the gravel road rose in the air like a dense cloud and then slowly drifted in the breeze toward the house. Khamiel hurried to close the windows before the fine white power covered everything in the house.

Leon's short visit and hasty departure disturbed her. "Why the sudden concern over Mother's research?"

"Maybe you should have asked him," Max's voice came from a hidden speaker.

"That was a rhetorical question, Max. One for which I do not expect an answer."

"Then why did you ask me?"

"The question was not directed to you." She crossed the kitchen and opened the access to the elevator.

"If there is no one in the room with you and you ask a question, it therefore must be directed to me."

Khamiel sighed. "Max, I was talking to myself." She entered the code and the elevator began to descend to the lab.

"Do you do this often?"

"Yes, I do." As she stepped out of the elevator, the lights came on. "Do you have a problem, Max?"

"I do not understand the question, Khamiel."

"Do you have a problem with the fact that I talk to myself?" The faint bleating of the ewe from the other room caught her attention.

"It is very...confusing."

The bleating increased. "Should I feed the sheep?"

"Are you asking me?"

"There's no one else here, is there?" Khamiel quipped.

A big yellow smiley face popped up on all the computer screens. Its eyes began to counter rotate. *"If my logic software fails, you will have no one to blame but yourself. Yes, you need to feed and water the sheep."*

"Does it have a name?" She started for the door.

"Number Ten."

"Why ten? What happened to one through nine?" Khamiel placed her hand on the doorknob.

"They died."

Khamiel felt a sinking sensation in the pit of her stomach as she entered the large storage area. She knew her mother hated testing on animals. Sometimes there was no other way...but nine failures? Had her mother's obsession with the project pushed her over the edge?

"Mother cried over the death of each one and would not work for days."

"Then why did she continue?" Khamiel went to the pen, reached in and the sheep nudged her hand. Almost instantly, the area where she touched changed color.

"The formula has to be part of the DNA for it to work. Simply washing the wool with it doesn't work."

She scratched behind the sheep's ears. "What was the problem with the first nine?"

"The temperature of the formula is critical. If allowed to increase before injection, it becomes unstable. Another problem was figuring out how much to inject into each animal."

Khamiel scooped food into a bucket and poured it in the feed pan. "Did Mother...experiment on any other animals?"

"Yes, Mother injected a guard dog."

"Oh, great!" she fumed. "There's an invisible dog running around here waiting to take a bite out of my ass."

"The dog died. Mother said it was poisoned."

"Was she sure?"

"Yes."

"What else did Mother experiment on?"

"She also did extensive research with cotton."

Her heart began to race with excitement. "Was she, successful?"

"She was still testing."

Khamiel turned the faucet on. "Explain." She picked up the hose and watered the sheep.

"Both materials appear to be body heat activated, but refuse to turn any other color than the skin tone of the person wearing it."

The water in the pan stirred as Number Ten began to drink.

Khamiel turned the water off and hung up the hose. "So...once the sheep is sheared, the wool looses some of the Chameleon properties. Max, did she find out why?"

"No. That is what she was working on when she took sick. Maybe if she had not let her assistant go, she would not have overworked herself."

"I didn't know Mother had an assistant." Khamiel reached into the pen, rubbed the sheep's head for a moment and then went back into the main lab.

"A Chinese girl named Lei Woo. Mother dismissed her three years ago. Immediately after she broke the Chameleon code."

"A vehicle is approaching."

Khamiel looked at the monitor and hurried to the elevator. As she entered the kitchen, she heard the car door shut. An elderly man with thick graying hair approached the house. He wore a pair of white long-sleeved coveralls and an isolation mask over his face. His shoulders slumped as if he carried the weight of the world on his back.

Unease ripped through Khamiel like the artic blast of a northeasterner. As she opened the door she fought to maintain an air of nonchalance. "Doctor Davidson, is that you? It's a little early for Halloween."

"Ms. Roche, may I come in?"

"Come in, please. Would you care for something to drink?"

"No, thank you." He took a seat, removed his breathing mask and wiped the beads of sweat from his forehead. "I'm sorry about your mother. She was a...dear friend of mine."

"I hadn't realized that. Thank you." Her hand shook as she poured herself a glass of water. There were two reasons why Doc would have removed his mask and the second was too horrific to contemplate. "What brings you all the way out here from Atlanta? Doesn't the big city have enough work to keep the Medical Examiner's Office busy?"

"I wanted to ask you some questions about your mother. Had she been out of the country recently?"

"Not that I'm aware of. If you were a friend of Mother's, then you know we sort of lost touch over the years." Khamiel took a drink. "Why do you ask?"

"As I'm sure you are aware, there is another new flu outbreak in China. About the time we get a vaccine for one, it mutates and we have to start over again. This new strain, H5N6, is so elusive and deadly that all travel to and from China has been forbidden."

She wanted the doc to leave without saying anything else. Khamiel dreaded the question she was about to ask, because she could see the answer in doc's eyes. "What does this have to do with my mother?"

The doctor rested his elbows on the table, laced his fingers together and rested his chin in his clasped hands. "There's no easy way to say this, Khamiel. Your mother tested positive for H5N6."

Khamiel shook her head in denial. "That's impossible!"

"Impossible or not, there's no mistake. CDC is on the way with a crew to try to locate the source of the H5N6 virus and disinfect the area. Of course, you and everyone who came in contact with your mother, including yours truly, will be in quarantine until we are positive that the threat no longer exists."

I was right. Doc wasn't trying to protect me with the mask, but those on the outside he came into contact with. We may both be already infected.

Doc's eyes misted with unshed tears. "I'm sorry Khamiel."

Khamiel felt a twinge of pity. She knew how the game was played. Doctor Davidson looked tired, but there would be little if any rest for him until the source of the virus was located.

A vehicle stopped in front of the house.

"That should be them now." The doctor sighed. "I'm really sorry to put you through all this, but it is necessary to prevent the spread of the virus."

Khamiel's mind reeled with the implications of his words. There had to be some mistake. Her home was about to be invaded, disinfected and sanitized from top to bottom. Could she keep them out of her mother's lab? If she couldn't, how was she going to explain the bleating of a sheep no one could see?

"Is something wrong, Khamiel? You look a little pale."

"I'm fine…this is so sudden and…overwhelming." She glanced toward the door wondering when the men in white suits were going to take over her world.

She went over to the door and opened it, expecting to find the CDC crew with their test equipment and sprayers. Instead, she saw the broad shoulders and back of a stranger dressed in a light blue shirt and jeans as he disappeared around the corner of her house.

Parked behind the doctors' BMW sat an old beat up pickup truck with several different sized ladders hanging on a rack. She glanced at the Medical Examiner and then to the truck.

Khamiel ran around the house after the stranger. She found him in back looking up at the weather-worn, peeling paint.

"Excuse me! What do you think you are doing?"

"Hello." His face lit up with a big wide, sexy smile. "I'm Stanley Freeman." He held out his hand. "Most people just call me Stan."

On instinct, Khamiel took his hand and then realized just what she had done. She quickly dropped it and clasped her hands together.

"Someone in town told me you might be in need of a painter." He turned his gaze back on the house. "This ol' place sure needs a lot of work. Looks like most of the wood is still in good shape, but it won't stay that way for long."

"I don't know where you got your information, but it's wrong. I think you need to leave immediately, Mr. Freeman."

"I'm afraid that isn't possible, Khamiel." Doctor Davidson leaned against the corner of the house. "For the next two weeks, neither of you are leaving quarantine."

"Quarantine! Just what the hell is going on around here?" Stan bellowed.

"I can't have a stranger hanging around here for two weeks." Khamiel placed both hands on her hips in defiance. "I do have my own life to live."

"Are you saying that I don't?" Stan fired back at her.

"No!"

There was something terrifying and stimulating in his fiery glare.

She faltered. "Of course not."

Doctor Davidson had a gleam of mischief in his eyes.

"You might as well make yourself useful, Mr. Freeman. I'm sure Doctor Davidson will make arrangements to have the paint you need delivered." She turned and headed for the front of the house. "There is running water in the barn, you can sleep there."

"I'll be damned if I'm sleeping in a barn," Stan huffed.

"CDC is going to set up shop in the barn, Khamiel," Doctor Davidson countered.

She could hear the laughter in his voice.

"Just where do you propose he..." She glanced from one man to the other.

"No!" She stomped her foot. "I absolutely forbid it."

She clinched her fingers into tight fists and marched off in a huff. "If you think for a minute that I'm going to allow a perfect stranger to move into my house, then you can both kiss my ass."

Stan watched her cute backside wiggle. As she disappeared around the corner of the house, he couldn't help but laugh. "She's a feisty little thing when she gets riled."

Davidson chuckled. "Like mother, like daughter."

"I heard in town her mother recently passed away. I take it you knew her mother well?"

The old man sighed and seemed hesitant to answer.

"Yes...I did."

Stan heard the anguish and regret in his voice.

"Mr. Freeman, you've walked into a difficult situation. One that involves a national health risk and is going to require you to stay here for several days. Why don't you wait out here while I see about getting you through the front door?"

Stan took a moment to ponder doc's statement. "Sure thing, Doc. I'll look the place over and figure out how much paint and material I'm going to need from town."

"You do that. I'll make sure you get everything you need." He started to walk away and stopped. "Please don't call anyone and mention this quarantine, Mr. Freeman. The last thing we need is to start a panic."

Khamiel knelt in the hay and scratched the sheep's head. Mother's death had turned her world upside down and now it was starting to come unraveled at the seams.

She heard the unmistakable whine of large motors kicking in and jumped to her feet. "Max! The elevator is moving."

"Yes it is."

It stopped and almost immediately started again.

"Do something, Max!" Panic rooted her feet to the floor.

The elevator opened and she heard slow footsteps in the main lab.

The doorknob slowly turned and the door between the two labs opened.

"I thought I'd find you in here." Doctor Davidson approached the pen. "I see you have met Number Ten."

She opened her mouth to speak, but no sound made it past her constricted throat.

"I'm sorry if seeing me here is such a shock, Khamiel." He leaned over and reached between the rails of the pen. Number Ten went straight to him. "I told your mother that she should have told you about us."

He petted the animal for a moment and then straightened. "She didn't think you would understand and feared it would complicate things."

"How could things get more complicated than they are right now?" Her legs suddenly felt like rubber and she sat on a pile of hay. "How long had you and...Mother been seeing each other?"

"Ever since my wife died four years ago, but I'd known her for years."

Number Ten, deciding it was time to play, knocked her over.

"Stop that." Khamiel pulled her legs underneath her, and as she started to get up, she got slammed in the ass with a head-butt. Back onto the floor she went, only this time it was to land face first in the watering pan.

She came up spitting water. "Damn you, Ten." Khamiel swiped at wet hair that was now plastered to her face.

Doc Davidson bent over holding his stomach. Tears ran freely down his face.

"Not one word from you, Doc. Not one damn word."

"Khamiel."

"Max, the same goes for you." She put her foot on a railing and swung her leg over. "Or I swear I'll pull your voice card."

Doc Davidson handed her a towel. "I better get back upstairs before I'm missed." He looked at his watch. "The CDC crew should be arriving any minute."

Khamiel toweled her hair. "Mr. Freeman can use my old room. I'll move my things into Mothers' room."

He left and a few moments later she heard the elevator take him back to the surface.

"Max, what other little secrets haven't you told me?"

"Like what, Khamiel?"

"Oh, I don't know. Like…it would have been nice to know that Doc Davidson had access before he came down and scared the crap out of me."

"If he did, you better go clean up before you go back upstairs."

"Max!" she fumed. "I didn't mean that literally. It was just a figure of speech.

"Bring up the access file."

The file opened on the screen and she stared at four access control numbers, but only three had names assigned.

"What the hell is this last set of numbers?"

"I don't know."

"What do you mean, you don't know?" Her fingers started flying over the keyboard. "Who put those numbers in the computer?"

"Mother."

"If there's no name, delete the fourth set of access codes. I can't seem to do it from the terminal."

"I am unable to do as requested. Mother set a security lock on it and a password on the information you want."

"You can't override them?"

"No."

"Damn Mother's paranoia." She stomped across the floor and into the elevator.

Khamiel entered her kitchen and came to an abrupt halt. Doc Davidson, with tongue in cheek, appeared to be interested in something on the ceiling and refused to look at her. Stan Freeman, who was just too damn good looking to be a house painter, sat at her kitchen table.

Whatever Doc was looking at didn't interest Stan one iota. His gaze at her could only be described as that of a pure predatory male–with a huge appetite.

The encounter with Ten's watering pan did more than get her face wet. Her shirt, now plastered to her skin, left nothing to the imagination.

"If you'll give me a few minutes, Mr. Freeman, I'll have my things moved out of the room." She maneuvered around the table. "Oh, in case you are wondering...these are breasts. I have two and they are both real. I'll tell you the same thing my mother told me when I was a little girl. Every time we went to the store she would say, 'you can look, but don't touch'."

Khamiel left the kitchen with as much poise as her disheveled attire allowed. She prided herself on not being a prude. She had long overcome being threatened by men's jokes and sexual innuendoes...so why did she feel so damn flustered?

Their laughter followed her down the hall.

She grabbed what few hanging clothes she had with her, carried them into her mother's bedroom and tossed them on the bed. "It's going to be a long two weeks."

A small computer screen lit up with a big grinning smiley face.

"Oh, shut up." She whirled around and walked into a rock solid wall of hot flesh.

Stan's arms went around her. "Need any help?"

For a brief moment she was floating, safe and secure, and then her sanity returned. Khamiel quickly backed away.

"No thank you. Why don't you just stay in the kitchen 'til I'm done? Do something useful and make a pot of coffee."

"Doc just made one."

"Then go make another." She went back to her old room. "Just stay out of my way."

Khamiel reached the bedroom door and gave a peek down the hall. Stan hadn't moved. The predatory glare was back, this time focused on her ass. Had she brushed up against something, or sat in a pile of sheep droppings? Her hand was reaching to check when she stopped herself.

Stan grinned.

The man infuriated her. *If only Leon were...* "Oh, my God!"

She turned and ran down the hall, bouncing off the wall as she went around Stan. "Doc! Doc! I almost forgot. A colleague of mine with the FBI, Leon Haufmyer, stopped by early this morning.

Doc sat at the table drinking a fresh brewed cup of coffee. He frowned and exhaled a long weary sigh. “This compounds the problem. He has to be isolated at once from the public. If this property is contaminated and he has come in contact with the virus, he won’t be contagious for a couple more days, but after that…”

He didn’t need to finish the sentence. She knew. The pandemic he was trying so hard to stop could spread like a wind-driven fire in dry grass.

Khamiel picked up the phone and dialed her office number.

A few minutes later, she slowly hung up the phone.

“Well?” Doc asked with anticipation in his voice.

“Leon missed his last contact time. He’s working undercover. They had no idea he’d left California or where he is now.”

She saw fear in Doc’s eyes. His hand shook. “Did he know about…?” His eyes quickly flickered to the floor and back.

“No…at least not that I’m aware of.”

“You two have lost me.” Stan glanced from one to the other. “What does this Leon fellow supposedly not know about?”

“Nothing,” they replied simultaneously.

“Doesn’t sound like nothing.”

“Mr. Freeman.” Khamiel softened her voice to hopefully take the sting out of her words. “It doesn’t concern you.”

Stan bristled. “I think it does. I came here to paint, not get caught up in a damn quarantine for two weeks.”

“In that case, Mr. Freeman, why don’t you get started?” She turned to face him and put her hands on her hips. “I’m sure you can find plenty to do outside.”

Dishes rattled on the shelf as Stan stomped across the floor.

"And, don't slam the—"

The door closed with a resounding crash.

"Door!"

Doc chuckled. "What I wouldn't give to be a fly on the wall these next two weeks."

Khamiel spun around and stormed down the hall. "Bite me."

"Oh, I think Stan can handle that all by himself."

She entered her old bedroom and swung the door closed with all her might. Her fingers tore at the buttons of her shirt. "Never have I met such an infuriating, conceited man in my life." Khamiel removed her shirt and tossed it at the clothesbasket.

Stan took that moment to set a stepladder in front of her window. His heated gaze bathed her naked breasts.

Doc was in the kitchen. She was on her own.

Her breathing increased. She licked her suddenly dry lips. "Do you mind?"

"Not one damn bit." His husky voice dripped with desire.

"Well I do." She crossed her arms over her breasts.

"Hey, I'm not the one getting undressed in front of an open window." Stan smiled and started up the ladder. "Besides, you said I could look."

"Well, that's all you will ever get to do." She dropped her arms and picked up a lacy bra. "So get a good look while you're able."

"Ms. Roche." He grinned. "Before I touch you, you'll have to beg for it." He ignored her, pulled his dust mask over his face and began scraping paint.

Khamiel fastened the bra, adjusted her breasts in the filmy cups and tugged a shirt over her head. She quickly finished moving her things to the other room.

If the bottom half looks as good as the top that little boast may be difficult to keep. "Very difficult indeed," he mumbled.

From his advantage point on the ladder, Stan watched the beehive of activity around the place. Two people searched the yard while two others checked the field and nearby woods. Another crew with sprayers converged on the barn. The door opened. Doctor Davidson went to the CDC van, removed a sprayer unit and returned to the house.

Stan felt a low vibration radiate through the old wooden structure. Curious, he climbed down the ladder. The locked door piqued his interest even more. With his back to the CDC van, Stan pulled a small, thin piece of metal from his wallet. He picked the lock on the door and went inside. A quick check of the house confirmed his suspicions.

Khamiel Roche and Doctor Davidson were gone.

Upon returning to the kitchen, Stan eyed the door Khamiel had used earlier to enter the room. When she had run blindly into his arms later in the hallway, she'd carried a heavy aroma of sheep on her clothes.

Stan smiled. He'd figured Doctor Marie Roche had played her hand close to her vest. Little had he realized just how close—until now.

Chapter Three

"Where do we start?" Khamiel stood in the center of the room and slowly turned around in a circle.

"You can give Number Ten a bath and wipe down all the rails of his pen." Doc handed her a bottle of disinfectant. "I'll work on the walls and floor. What we're using isn't as harsh as what they are using outside. We won't need respirators."

She laughed. "Why did I even bother changing? I'll end up as wet as Ten."

"Because you didn't like the way Stan was looking at you." Doc headed toward the other section of the underground lab.

"That's *bull.*" She caught up to him. "And you're full of it."

He pointed to a double-door steel locker. "That cabinet contains your mother's lab smocks."

"I just met the man. Why should I care how I look or what he thinks?" Khamiel opened the locker and peeled her shirt over her head. "Go ahead and get started. I'll just be a minute."

Doc averted his eyes but his voice sparkled with mischief. "If you couldn't care less about the guy, then why the fancy lace?"

She undid her pants, stepped out of them and reached for the closest white lab coat. As she touched it, a light golden brown color spread across the material. Khamiel grabbed it off the hanger and ran into the other room.

“Doc! Doc! It’s the Chameleon material. It’s amazing.”

He laughed. “Yeah, it is that.” Doc paused his spraying and leaned against the pen railing. “You might want to put it on before Number…”

A sudden jerk pulled the smock from her hands and it disappeared. Left standing naked, except for a pair of red lace panties and matching bra, Khamiel bounded over the pen railing.

“Ten! Stop that right now.” She groped blindly around the pen trying to find the sheep. “Give me back my smock.”

She could hear the rustle of feet across the floor and see the stirring of the loose straw, but every time she lunged, she came up empty handed. “Damn!”

Khamiel sat on the floor and pulled straw out of her hair. “A big help you are.”

Doc, doubled over in laughter, leaned heavily on the pen’s top rail. “Funniest…thing I’ve…seen.” His right hand slapped the rail.

Her white lab coat appeared on the floor a couple feet in front of her. She slowly pulled her feet underneath her, lunged for it and ended up having to spit straw out of her mouth. “Forget it.”

Khamiel climbed to her feet and left the pen. “How am I supposed to get the coat back, much less wash a damn sheep I can’t see?”

Doc handed her a pair of infrared goggles. “Here, this might help. I’ll turn the lights down.”

The lights dimmed and she pulled the goggles over her head. It took a moment for her eyes to adjust to the green light. “Ok, Ten. Playtime is over.” She slowly approached the sheep with her arms outstretched. “You can run, but you can’t hide.”

Ten stood perfectly still and dropped the lab coat as she approached. Khamiel picked up the material and took the goggles off. “Okay, Doc, you can turn the lights up.

She slipped her arms into the sleeves and buttoned the coat. “I had the strangest feeling that Ten knew I could see her.”

“I guess we’ll never know for sure.” Doc picked up the sprayer and paused. “Khamiel, you’re a beautiful woman and—” his voice caught, “—so much like your mother. Don’t put off finding happiness. One of these days, you’ll end up like me...old and alone.”

“What’s that supposed to mean?” She watched him for several seconds.

“Nothing, just the ramblings of an old fool.”

You loved her, but couldn’t compete with her world. The thought gave her a pause of reflection. Khamiel stepped over to the faucet, began filling a bucket with water and added the concentrated disinfectant. *Neither could I.*

“Okay, Ten.” She carried the bucket to the pen and set it over the rail. “It’s time for a bath.”

She squatted down, took a brush and began scrubbing Ten’s wool. “That’s a good girl. Just stand still and this will soon be over.”

Doc laughed. “Max, put her on the monitor.”

Khamiel looked up. A picture of the pen came on screen. Her head and hands were the only things visible.

"That's amazing—but it sure gives me a weird feeling. Must be something in the material that recognizes the Chameleon DNA within the sheep."

"Marie worked on that theory up until she took sick." Doc paused by the pen. "She just couldn't prove it, or explain why—on paper."

"She always did have problems with accepting things at their face value." Khamiel sighed. "I might as well clean this pen while I'm here."

"I'll start in the other room." Doc winked. "You might want to get cleaned up before you leave. Stan could get the wrong idea if you look like you've had a roll in the hay."

"Why should I care what he thinks?"

Doc had a twinkle in his eye. "No reason that I can think of."

"I need to rinse this water-logged ball of wool." She set the bucket aside. "Would you hand me the hose and turn the water on, please?"

An hour later, soaked and covered with straw dust, Khamiel left the pen. "I'm all done in here."

Doc stuck his head through the doorway and started laughing.

She turned the bucket over and sat down. "I'm not sure who got wetter, Ten or me."

"Get a shower. I'm going up to check with the CDC team." Doc picked up his sprayer and left.

Khamiel stripped off her lab coat, hung it up to drip dry and trudged over to the lab's emergency shower. She adjusted the temp and stepped underneath the pulsating spray.

She leaned against the shower stall. "Max, what am I going to do?"

"Regarding what, Khamiel?"

"Mother's work." She sighed. "What am I going to do with the lab and with Ten?"

"What do you want to do?"

"I don't know." Khamiel closed her eyes and let the water and steam envelope her. "I have my own life...a career. If I do nothing, all the years of her research will have been for nothing."

"I can give you the recipe for some soothing tea."

She laughed and turned off the shower. "I don't think tea will help right now."

"When Mother had questions she couldn't answer, she would go pet Number Ten."

"Thanks just the same, but I've had quite enough of her today." Khamiel took a towel and dried off. She picked up her panties and bra, shook her head at their sad demise and tossed them into a trashcan.

"Max, bring the kitchen up on the monitor." She wiggled her butt into a pair of pants. "I don't need a repeat of earlier."

"Max, bring up the outside cameras."

The picture changed and flashed rapidly across several different locations.

"Stop...now go back to the last camera."

"Can you zoom in?"

The camera lens moved in closer. She felt a sense of exhilaration at being able to watch Stan without being seen.

Something just didn't look right. For someone being tossed into the middle of a medical quarantine, her painter seemed relaxed. At the speed he moved, he didn't appear in a hurry to get anything done. He might have looked busy to a casual observer, but she thought he spent way too much time keeping an eye on everyone else.

"Thank you, Max."

About to turn out the lights, Khamiel paused, went back to the pen and stuck her hand over the railing. The stirring of straw brought a smile to her face. Ten nuzzled her hand and she scratched its woolly head. "Goodnight, my invisible friend."

Baa.

She walked back to the elevator humming Mary Had A Little Lamb.

Back in the kitchen, Khamiel poured a cup of coffee, took a sip and screwed up her face. The contents of the cup went into the sink, followed by the remainder of the pot.

The outside door opened. "You don't like my coffee?" Doc came in and removed his mask.

"Is that what that was?" She filled the pot with fresh water. "I thought maybe this was the disinfectant CDC is using outside."

"Tsk, Tsk." Doc shook his head. "You Northerners just don't have an appreciation for good Southern coffee."

"Next, I suppose you are going to tell me my mother drank this boiled swamp bark." She took a filter and added new grounds.

"She acquired a taste for it." He sat at the kitchen table.

"Humph." *It had to be love.*

An uneasy silence settled over the kitchen. The ticking of the clock grew louder. Water flowing through the coffee pot sounded like a faucet left open. The continuous scrape, scrape, scrape on the side of the house ate at her nerves. She started to pace the length of the kitchen.

"That's not going to help."

"I feel so damn helpless." She glared at the coffee pot.

"I know." Doc exhaled a long sigh.

The door opened and Stan entered the kitchen. "Now, that smells like coffee."

"At least we agree on something." She laughed. "How's it going?"

He sat beside Doc. "Not too bad. I've seen worse."

Stan's eyes caressed her from head to toe and she felt self-conscious.

"What's the chance of getting something to eat around here," he asked with a smile. "I'm so hungry I could eat a sheep—wool and all."

Doc coughed.

Khamiel quickly turned around to avoid Stan's eyes. She reached for a clean cup and the coffee pot. Her hands shook. The cup overflowed.

Stan jumped up. "Why don't you sit down and I'll clean that up. Then you can tell me where everything is and I'll make lunch."

"I'm fine." She wiped up the spilt coffee and shoved a cup into his hand. "If you really want to help, just go get cleaned up and I'll throw something together.

"Doc." She lifted the pot off the counter. "Do you want some?"

“You threw out the good stuff.” Doc pushed out of the chair. “I’m going to the barn and see how the tests are going.”

Stan left the kitchen and she rushed over to Doc. “You’re going to abandon me?”

“You’re a big girl.” He chuckled. “If he attacks you with his pickle, you can beat him off with a loaf of bread.”

Khamiel laughed despite her mood. “You’re a big help.”

Doc left. She opened the refrigerator door and looked in dismay at the nearly empty shelves. “There has to be something in this house to eat.”

She pulled hotdogs and buns out of the freezer, set them on the counter and began filling a pan with water.

“Find something?”

Khamiel jumped. Water splashed out of the pan and covered her shirt.

Stan laughed. “Sorry, didn’t mean to startle you.” He grabbed a towel and started blotting the water from her top.

“What...what do you think you’re doing?” She froze as his hand brushed the underside of her breast. Her stomach tightened. Heat pooled between her legs, warming her with an alarming desire.

“Helping.”

She swallowed. “I’m quite capable of doing it myself, thank you.”

“Do I make you nervous?”

“Yes, a little.” She forced her legs to take a step back.

“Sorry, that was not my intention. Why don’t you sit down and I’ll fix these.” He poured her a cup of coffee.

Khamiel sat and watched him. There wasn't much skill required to boil hotdogs, but something in his movements told her he was comfortable, sure of himself in a kitchen.

Her gaze dropped to his hands. "You're not married, are you?"

"No." He stuck the frozen buns in the microwave with a little more force than necessary.

"Why not?" She took a sip. Khamiel held the cup between both hands as she watched him through the rising steam.

"I move around a lot." The buzzer sounded on the microwave.

"Let me guess...you worked your way through college painting houses and working as a short order cook. You got tired of the corporate scene and turned your back on a nine to five, high paying career in a crowded city to do something you enjoy."

Stan chuckled. "Something like that."

He opened the refrigerator door and stared. "I hope you plan on sending out a grocery list. Otherwise we might starve in the next two weeks."

"I'll see if I can fit it into my busy schedule."

He placed the food on the table and straddled a chair. "Tell me something, Ms. Roche..."

"Please, we might as well be informal. My name is Khamiel." She took another sip of coffee.

"As in Chameleon?"

She choked on the coffee and started coughing. "Sorry, must have gone down the wrong pipe."

A paper towel was thrust toward her face. "Are you okay?"

"Yes." She took the towel and cleared her throat. "Yes, I am. Thank you."

Stan lips formed a slight smile. “Good, I’m a little rusty on my CPR.”

I bet you have the mouth-to-mouth down perfect. She stuffed a hot dog in her mouth and took a huge bite.

“You must’ve worked up an appetite this morning.” Stan quirked an eyebrow in an accusing arch, as if he knew exactly what she had been doing. “There’s more in the pan.”

Thankfully, a mouth full of food kept her from answering immediately.

Stan never shifted his gaze from her.

She swallowed.

“So, Khamiel, how much more *cleaning* do you have to do?”

Stan’s penetrating gaze gave her an uneasy feeling. Her food settled like a rock in her stomach. She glanced over to the sprayer. “Oh, just a little bit more.”

“Funny...” he followed her glance, “...I wouldn’t think it would take so long to do the inside. It’s not that big of a house. Come to think of it, I didn’t hear any noise or see any movement through the windows while I was scraping paint.”

“We were...ah...in the basement.” The rock in the pit of her stomach grew. “Mother spent a lot of time down there.”

“Really—I didn’t realize this old house had a basement.” Stan smiled as he sat down and started eating.

“You must have been down there when I tried to get a drink, but the door was locked,” he said as he lifted his cup to his lips.

“Oh!” she feigned surprise. “I’m sorry. I wonder how it got locked.”

The muscles in Stan’s cheek twitched. “Difficult to say.”

Khamiel got up from the table.

"You haven't finished." His eyes shifted to her plate.

"As you reminded me," she said as she picked up the sprayer, "I have things to do."

Panic lent wings to her feet as she hurried down the hall. She went into the bathroom, closed the doors to the connecting bedrooms and sat on the edge of the tub. *What am I going to do? He knows about the lab—I know he does...but how?*

Her fear grew. Who could she turn to for help? Doc? He was an old man. What could he do?

The CDC team? Khamiel shook her head. They were technicians, scientists looking for a virus. Beside that, she doubted any of them were armed.

"If only Leon were here."

She remembered Max's warning...Stan's sudden appearance at the house and his watchfulness as she spied on him. Then there were his off-handed comments about sheep, her name and the door to the elevator.

"I have to protect Mother's work."

Stan finished eating, put the dishes in the sink and went outside. He squinted against the blaring hot summer sun and removed his shirt. A faint bitter chemical odor still hung in the air and bit at the tender lining of his nose. "A breeze would sure be nice."

He moved the ladder to the backside of the house where he would be out of the direct rays from the sun and went back to work.

Khamiel took a couple of deep breaths as she tried to gain control of her emotions and still her shaking hands. She stood, opened the door to her mother's room and tiptoed to the bed. As she searched through her pile of clothes, she listened for any clue to Stan's location. With a sigh of relief, she closed her fingers around the handle of her FBI issue revolver.

What am I doing? I'm an analyst not a damn field agent.

Khamiel heard a noise outside the window and ducked down below the bed. Her palms became slick with sweat. She wiped each hand on her pants leg and tried to control her rapid breathing. Ever so slowly, she peeked around the corner of the bed.

Stan stood on the ladder with his head above the window giving her an unexpectedly intriguing view. The muscles in his chest rippled like well-choreographed dancer's. Paint chips, like glitter, stuck to his damp skin. His jeans hung low on his waist. He stretched and his waistband shifted.

Her gaze dropped to a small round puckered scar at the edge of the material. A bullet wound, of that she had no doubt. Frightened and confused, she slowly lifted her revolver toward the window.

"Mr. Freeman... FBI... Don't move!"

Chapter Four

Stan heard the quiver of fear in her voice. He felt his gut tighten. After living on the edge, one develops a sixth sense to impending danger and his was screaming at him to move. He dove off the ladder and caught a glimpse of Khamiel pointing a handgun at the window.

The window erupted in a spray of flying glass and noise.

“Damn it, woman! Have you lost your frigging mind?” He rolled against the house, got into a crouch and ran to the corner of the building.

The kitchen door slammed.

Stan heard her slow careful footsteps as she approached the corner where he waited.

She stopped.

The muscles in his legs tensed like coiled springs.

Khamiel jumped around the corner holding her weapon with both hands in front of her.

He sprang from his position, came in low under her arms and deflected the barrel into the air. His shoulder slammed into her ribcage and he heard her grunt as they hit the ground.

Her face twisted in agony. She lay unmoving beneath him.

Stan twisted the gun from her hand and gave it a toss.

For some strange reason, he thought that would be the end of it and he let her go.

He was wrong.

From out of nowhere, a foot connected with his gut, catching him off guard. Khamiel clawed at the ground toward her weapon.

"Damn!" Stan scrambled after her. He lunged, wrapped his arms around her waist and they rolled across the grass.

He landed on top of her and pinned her arms to the ground above her head. In the tussle, her top had ridden up over her heaving breasts.

His reaction was instant and hard.

She bucked and twisted beneath him.

I've got two choices. I can knock her out or try something desperate—He kissed her hard on the mouth.

Khamiel went stock-still. All movements ceased except for the rapid rise and fall of her breasts.

"If I let you go, will you promise not to shoot me?"

"How do you know about the Chameleon project?"

"From your mother."

She lunged. "That's a damn lie!"

Their positions reversed, Stan looked up at the sky as she straddled his hips. Her weapon lay within easy reach.

"Who the hell are you?" she snarled.

Maybe I should have gone with the first choice. "Agent Stanley Freeman, NSA, Field Commander, Special Projects Division."

"Why should I believe you?"

He couldn't stop staring at her. Kissing her had been a mistake. Now, he wanted to do it again and not just on the lips.

"Would you stop gawking at my breasts?"

Stan smiled and looked into her eyes. "That would be like asking an art lover to not look at a Rembrandt."

"You need to either have your eyes checked, or take an art class. Answer my question.

He laughed. "Check the ID in my wallet."

"ID's can be faked."

"Call the NSA office in Washington, D.C. and when they ask for an extension, use the special access code in your computer. The number you will be given is the password to unlock your mother's files."

"Wrong answer," she snarled. "How about you give me the access code—then I'll call."

"Fair enough, 1...8...5...4...0."

Her shoulders slumped.

"I see those numbers aren't new to you."

She shook her head. "Okay, I promise I won't shoot you. Unless I have to."

"Wow, that's a comforting thought." He let go of her wrists. "To prove I'm the good guy here, you can pick up your weapon. Do me one favor, don't point it at me again. I have an aversion to getting shot."

She pulled her top down. "I take it once was enough," Khamiel said wryly as she picked up her revolver. "I saw the scar when you were on the ladder."

Stan got up and winced when he took a step. He lowered his hand to his waistband. "Would you like to see the other one?"

"Ah...no that's quite all right."

He snickered at her reddening face. “Cute, a blushing FBI agent.”

“Ha, ha, very funny.” She stood, stuck the revolver in the waistband of her pants and started toward the house. For the moment, she was buying his story although she wasn’t sure why. “We have a phone call to make.”

“Aren’t you afraid I’ll sneak up from behind and take you?” He followed behind her, watching the sexy wiggle of her ass.

“Don’t think for a minute I didn’t feel how aroused you were. I figure if you were gentleman enough not to take advantage of me then, I can trust you to keep your end of the bargain.”

“What about the kiss we shared?” He stepped ahead of her and opened the door.

“*Shared* my foot.” She sashayed past him. “You *stole* that kiss.”

He pulled the door to, kicked off his shoes and followed her down the hall. “May I steal another?”

“No!” She entered her mother’s old bedroom and pulled down the door to an antique oak secretary desk. “What’s the number?”

She took her revolver from her waistband and set it on a shelf.

Inside the cabinet, he saw a keyboard, small monitor and a camera. “I could tell you any number. Call information and get it. Area code is...”

“I *know* what the area code is.”

Stan sat on the edge of the bed and bounced a of couple times. “Nice and comfy.”

She ignored him, picked up the phone and dialed.

"Washington, D.C. NSA." She waited for the number and then hit one for automatic dial.

"Don't forget to write it down."

She glared at him. *One more word out of you, mister, and I'm going to stick this phone where the sun doesn't shine.* The ringing stopped and she listened to the long computerized greeting. With pen in hand, she dialed in the code.

Almost instantly, she heard a familiar female voice on the other end of the line. She jotted down the numbers and the line went dead.

Khamiel looked at the receiver, then at Stan. "That...was the *president.*"

"You can hang up the phone now."

Dazed, she put the receiver back into its cradle. "Stan, would you sit here, face the camera and hold still."

He got up from the bed and placed the chair in front of the lens. "Didn't you ever wonder where your mother came up with this *toy*?" Stan removed his ID badge from his billfold and handed it to her.

"Plenty of times, but she wouldn't tell me.

"Max, bring up access file, 1...8...5...4...0."

A gray box came up on the screen with the words "Enter Password" flashing in red. Khamiel turned the keyboard to her and began typing, 9...0...7...4...1...5.

"Facial recognition scan in progress, insert verification card."

She inserted his ID badge into a small black box and waited.

"Please don't move, Agent Freeman. This is almost over."

Stan waited patiently as he mentally counted off the thirty seconds required to complete the initial scan.

"Welcome to Project Chameleon, Agent Freeman."

She handed Stan his ID and closed the secretary. "I imagine you would like to see the lab."

"Sure," he smiled, "but first you owe me an apology for trying to shoot me."

"I am sorry about that. I guess some of Mother's paranoia rubbed off on me. All I could think about was protecting her work."

"Not good enough." He lifted his hand and tapped his finger on his left cheek.

"You've got to be kidding." Khamiel moved away from the desk.

"Hey, a verbal apology would be sufficient for something as simple as spilling my coffee or burning breakfast, but shooting at a person is pretty extreme. I think that calls for a tremendous gesture on your part." Stan tapped his cheek again.

Khamiel lifted her hands in the air. "I don't believe this." She stepped forward, leaned over and closed her eyes.

Stan turned his face at the last second and her lips met his.

She broke the kiss, but didn't move away. "That's cheating."

"No," he whispered. "It's not." He lifted his hand to the back of her head and gently applied pressure. "This is cheating."

Hot burning desire surged through him. The taste of her lips was a potent drug and he was already an addict. Stan deepened the kiss. He felt her respond and then quickly push away from him.

"I can't do this."

Her ragged breathing matched his own. He saw the swirl of desire and the cloud of confusion within her eyes. "You're right. We must remain professional. And besides, it's too soon."

"Exactly." Her tongue traced the fullness of her lips. "Way too soon."

"Before I see the lab, I'd like to get cleaned up a bit," he said as he pushed out of the chair.

"Oh! I forgot. The bathroom hasn't been wiped down yet." Khamiel hurried out of the bedroom. "I'll just be a few minutes."

"Fine, I'll be in my room. Just knock on the door when you're finished."

Stan went into his room and laid out a change of clothes. He removed his pants, shorts and socks, and then picked up his shaving kit.

His first kiss shocked her and his second, a teasing dare. *So, why did I stick around and invite the third?*

Khamiel worked furiously cleaning the bathroom, but couldn't get the thought or taste of his last kiss off her mind.

She finished and slowly surveyed the room. "Why am I doing this?" she whispered. "Why am I even thinking about this?" *Because, Leon is nothing more than a good time in bed—when he's not with someone else.*

"I don't need this right now." She opened the door to Stan's room.

"All..." her gaze dropped to his cock and then she gasped, "...done." A large ugly scar ran from his waist to his right knee.

He frowned. "You were supposed to knock."

"My God, Stan, what happened?"

"Someone ran out of paper targets and used me instead." He walked toward her.

"Stop being a cynical smart-ass and tell me." She blocked his path.

"Excuse me." Stan pushed past her, laid his shaving kit on the sink and stepped into the shower.

"Stanley Freeman—"

"I don't want your pity." He cut her off, closed the shower curtain and turned the water on.

Khamiel flung the curtain open. "I wasn't giving any." She stepped into the shower. "I want to know what happened."

"You're getting all wet."

"Damn it, quit changing the subject," she fumed as she tugged her top over her head and tossed it over the shower curtain.

Wanton, naked desire filled the large black pupils of his piercing blue eyes. His nostrils flared as his chest swelled.

Disturbed by his passion, she lowered her gaze and smiled. "You don't seem to be adversely affected from your trauma."

"After weeks in a hospital and months in physical therapy...being this close to you—" He lifted his hand to her face and his fingers trailed sensuously down her jaw.

She gently touched each round puckered scar before sliding along the purplish incision. "Tell me what happened...please."

"An assignment gone bad." He shrugged. "Wrong place, wrong time or misinformation. All I know for sure is, when the bullets stopped flying—I had one 9 mm hollow point in the side, two in the hip. The fourth shattered my leg. I came out of surgery nine hours later with a Titanium hip and femur, and twenty pounds heavier."

She put her arms around him. "And then I put you through hell today. I'm so sorry, Stan." With her breasts flattened against his broad chest, she felt more alive than she had in months—maybe years.

"Hey, don't go hysterical on me and start crying." He kissed the top of her head. "The doctors released me for full duty. If I can't handle rolling around in the grass with a beautiful woman, I better hand in my badge and take up playing pool."

Khamiel wiggled against him and laughed. "You must be pretty good at it. You have your own stick."

He tipped her chin up and looked longingly into her eyes. "I haven't played since the shooting."

"Surely a man of your abilities could find a table to play on." She stood on tiptoe to bring her lips closer to his.

"I never found one worth the challenge of the game—until now."

His lips touched hers in a soft feather-light kiss, which promised more than it gave. By following him into the shower, she had thrown herself at him. Yet, he held back. The decision was up to her. She could still turn and walk away.

Chapter Five

Khamiel leaned against the shower wall. She knew in her heart this would be a high stakes game.

Doc's words from earlier that day came to her. *"Don't put off finding happiness. One of these days, you'll end up like me...old and alone...old and alone...old and alone."*

"I—I want to play."

He lifted his right hand and touched the side of her neck. "You don't sound very convincing." He glided his fingers down her wet skin and stopped short of touching her breast.

She unsnapped her pants with trembling fingers and let them fall to the floor. "*Please*, touch me."

"I thought you'd never ask."

Stan's electrifying touch sent a jolt from her nipple to her very core. Her legs weakened and her knees buckled. His left arm went around her waist and pulled her against his lean hard body. Their lips touched in a demanding tongue-probing kiss.

"Oh, wow," she moaned in a breathless sigh. *And to think, I almost walked out the door.*

He turned the water off, opened the curtain and picked her up in his arms. Khamiel put her arms around his neck and he carried her into his bedroom.

"Did I tell you how beautiful you are?" He kissed her.

"Yes." She ran her fingers through his short blond hair. "But don't let that stop you from telling me again. Every woman wants to hear she is beautiful, even if she doesn't think it's true."

He smiled as he knelt on the bed and slowly lowered her to the mattress, "I think you are very beautiful."

"You're not so bad yourself," she whispered.

As she lowered her hand down the length of his arm, her fingernails lightly scratched his skin. The sensation was so overpowering he nearly lost control.

Stan snorted as he stretched out beside her. "It will be a long time before I go to the beach again. I know what this looks like."

"Stanley Freeman," she scolded as she sat up in the bed, "stop with the self-pity."

Khamiel leaned over and kissed the scar where it ended at his knee. "You could've quit." She kissed it again further up the leg. "Given up." She placed another kiss on the scar at his hip. "But you didn't."

Her lips caressed each round puckered scar where hot lead had ripped through his body and shattered his life. "I see this as a badge of courage."

His body tensed as her fingers played in the curly blond hair surrounding his erect cock. Khamiel smiled, turned her head and kissed its wet shiny head.

Stan grasped the sheets in tight clutching fists. His body jerked and his hips lifted from the bed.

She parted her lips and let his motion push his cock into her mouth.

"Ahhh!" His passionate moan filled the room.

Khamiel sat up, licked her lips and swung her leg across his hips.

"What are you doing?" He started to sit up.

"I thought you might need a quick refresher course." She pushed him back down to the bed. "Don't worry, I've had all my shots."

"I wanted our first time to be special."

Khamiel rose up on her knees and grasped his cock. "Trust me." She placed the head of his hard shaft inside her pussy. "It's going to be *very* special." Ever so slowly, she lowered her body and took him inside.

His eyebrows lifted, his pupils grew dark and stormy. Stan parted his lips and his raspy gasp sounded like an out of tune violin string.

Khamiel smiled, tightened her inner muscles and his head came off the pillow. "That was the one ball in the side pocket."

"Do that again," he panted, "and it'll be the eight ball—game over."

"Well," she purred, "if that happens, we'll just have to rack the balls for a new game." Ever so slowly, Khamiel began to rotate her hips.

His hands moved across the sheet, up her sides and covered her breasts.

Khamiel closed her eyes as the pleasure of his cock swept over her. "Mmm," she moaned. *I think I wanted this as much as you did, but for completely different reasons.*

To hell with Leon, it was over. It was past time that she realized he would never change, no matter how long she waited. He was on track to self-destruct and she wanted off the train.

What better way to exorcise an ex-lover than to have wild passionate sex with someone who, at least on the outside, seemed to genuinely care about her feelings and desires?

“Ahh! Come join the party, Khamiel. You’re a million miles away.”

“Wool gathering over.” She smiled. “I’m all yours.”

Chapter Six

"Are you ready to see Mother's laboratory?"

"Sure, why not." He swung his feet out of bed and reached for his jeans. "Maybe seeing the lab for myself will help answer some of my questions."

"What kind of questions?"

"Well, for one..." He paused a moment. "Why didn't your mother come forward to accept the most coveted honor a person could ever hope to receive in a lifetime?"

"Oh!" Her eyes widened in surprise. "Which honor are you referring to?"

"You're kidding." Stan laughed.

"I haven't a clue what you are talking about."

"The Nobel Peace Prize." He watched confusion spread across her face. "For finding the AIDS Vaccine." He stood and finished dressing.

She sat on the edge of the nightstand.

"Don't tell me you didn't know."

Her head slowly moved back and forth. "I had no idea. How did you find out?"

"I twisted some arms and got her file opened." He motioned toward the door. "I'm ready when you are."

Khamiel scrambled into a pair of shorts and tugged a top over her head.

"Whose arms did you have to twist?" She stood and walked out the door.

Stan chuckled. "The president's."

"Oh!"

He followed Khamiel into the kitchen.

She stopped in front of the pantry door. "This is the entrance to the lab."

"I figured that one out," he said with a smirk.

"If it won't open." She ignored his jibe and opened the door. "Push in on the handle to call the elevator back to this level."

Khamiel showed him the control panel. "Enter your access code here. As soon as Max verifies it's you, the elevator will take you down to the lab."

"This is the only entrance?"

"The only one with direct access from ground level." She smiled as she pulled the door closed. "I'll see you down below."

Stan waited until the low vibration stopped and then pushed the doorknob. A few moments later, he opened the door, stepped into the elevator and slid back the cover for the hidden control panel.

"There wasn't this much damn security at the White House," he mumbled.

"That is where you are incorrect, Agent Freeman. The White House utilizes the same security measures for the president's underground facilities."

"I hope her elevator is bigger."

"That I do not know."

The elevator stopped and he opened the door to a world of white, stainless steel and florescent lights. "Wow! This is some layout."

Khamiel took his hand and led him between two long rows of counters filled with scientific test equipment. "Do you know what you are looking at?"

"No, but it all looks impressive."

"You ain't seen nothing yet." She stopped in front of the double-door cabinet. "Close your eyes."

He looked around the room.

"Go on. I want this to be a surprise."

Stan grinned and closed his eyes. He heard her open the cabinet.

"No peeking." She then took his hand and led him away.

His shoulder brushed a door jam. Instantly, the odor of straw, manure and sheep assaulted his senses.

"Keep them closed."

Baa, Baa!

"It sounds like someone is happy to see you. I know...no peeking."

Khamiel let go of his hand. "Stand here and wait."

Each second that passed, his anticipation increased.

"Okay, Stan, you can open your eyes."

He blinked, looked around and slowly turned in a circle. "Okay, where did you go?"

She giggled.

Stan spun around and faced the empty pen.

Baa!

In a daze of bewilderment, he leaned on the railing. "*Khamiel?*"

"I'm right here." Her head appeared like magic. "Come on over, I'd like for you to meet Number Ten."

"It does exist."

"Of course, it does."

"The president had the highest regard for you mother, but even she had doubts." He climbed over the rail and shuffled cautiously toward her. "I...don't want to step on it or you."

"You won't." Khamiel extended her hand to him. "She's right here beside me."

He knelt beside her and she placed his hand on Ten's back.

"I can hear it, feel it and even smell it...but I can't see it except where I'm touching it. This is absolutely amazing. I can't wait to tell the president. The camouflage works perfectly."

She released her hold on Ten and stepped back. "No, it doesn't." The lab coat turned light tan.

"But, I just saw it," he protested. "It works."

"Sorry, Stan." She removed the lab coat and tossed it over the railing. "For some reason the material has to come in contact with a live carrier of the DNA in order to blend in."

"Oh." He sat on the floor and ran his hand down the sheep's side. "So, it's not much use for designing new camouflage."

"Afraid not." She sat beside him.

"I do have some good news," Stan said in a serious tone of voice. "She's about ready to drop a lamb."

"What!" Khamiel jumped to her feet. "How do you know?"

"My family had sheep, or my granddad did." He felt along Ten's swollen belly.

"When is she due?" Khamiel paced across the pen.

"It's been some time since I played midwife. Could be tonight...or a week, it's difficult to tell for sure, but I don't foresee any problems."

She ran her fingers through her hair. "I need a drink."

"Come on, it's not that bad." Stan stood and brushed the straw from his jeans.

"Not that bad!" She stopped pacing and faced him. "What the hell am I going to do with a herd of invisible sheep in the city?"

He shrugged his shoulders. "I don't know, maybe we could train them to be secret agents and when they catch the bad guys they could wooly them to jail."

Khamiel cringed at his bad joke. "What happened, they throw you out of the Improv, so you decided to become an agent?"

With a theatrical swoon, Stan fell to his knees and crossed his wrists over his heart. "Thy words doth pierce my soul."

Baa!

A hard force plowed into his back and drove him face down on the floor.

Khamiel helped him stand. "Let's get out of here before Ten puts the wooly cuffs on you for practicing Shakespeare without a license."

"Marlowe," he corrected.

"Marlowe, who?" She climbed over the railing.

"Christopher Marlowe." He followed her over the railing. "From the play, *Tamburlaine the Great*."

She shrugged her shoulders. "Did this Marlowe fellow have any suggestions on what to do with sheep?"

Stan thought for a moment. "Not that I'm aware of. He was a poet."

"Then I'm right back where I started." She looked at the pen and shook her head. "You can stay down here and play midwife if you want to." Khamiel turned toward the door. "I'm going to find Doc Davidson. If he knew about Number Ten being pregnant and didn't tell me, I'm going to box his ears."

"I don't think I'm needed here just yet." He grinned behind her back. "But I'll put the water on to boil just in case."

She turned her head. "You have to do that with sheep too?"

"Oh, sure." He tried to keep a straight face.

"When you get the water hot—" Khamiel opened the elevator door and stepped in, "—soak your head in it."

She closed the elevator door to the sound of his laughter.

It's been a day from hell. I don't know what I'd have done without Stan. Thank goodness, I didn't shoot him. She smiled. *Especially after that fantastic sex.* "Wow! I need to figure out how to keep him around after CDC leaves, maybe he can paint the barn too."

"Khamiel."

"Not that he would get much painting done."

"Khamiel."

"Yes, Max." The elevator stopped and she paused with her hand on the doorknob.

"What are you thinking?"

"Why do you ask?"

"You have the same expression on your face as Mother did after Doc Davidson would spend the night."

"Ahh...Thanks, Max, I really needed to know that information."

"You're welcome, Khamiel."

"I'm glad there are no cameras in the bedrooms," she mumbled.

"There are, but Mother unplugged them. Why would she do that?"

"Gee, Max, I really don't know." As she left the elevator, Khamiel made a mental note to confine sex to bedrooms only.

She left the house and looked around in surprise at how much of the day had passed. Khamiel started down the path. Footsteps sounded behind her and she turned. "I thought I'd walk with you down to the barn." Stan fell in beside her. "I need to find something to board up that broken window."

Two cars blocked the main road. There were two more parked beside the barn. A man stood facing the structure, feet spread with one arm braced against the building. He looked over his shoulder, straightened and hurried inside.

"I hope he finished." She giggled.

"That's the advantage of wearing black trousers." He wiggled his eyebrows. "You can piss yourself without anyone else knowing. Course, you have to stay down wind."

She took hold of his arm. "You know that from firsthand experience?"

His voice sobered. "Yeah, I do."

A mental picture of Stan's body covered in blood and lying on the cold hard ground, flashed through her mind.

"Hey, you two." Doc Davidson stepped out of the barn and waved. "What brings you slumming down here?"

"I broke a window," Stan answered before she had a chance to. "I need to board it up until I can get a new pane for it."

"We heard a shot earlier, everything okay?" Doc shifted his gaze between them.

Khamiel thought quickly. "I...ah dropped my weapon and was checking to make sure it was still sighted in."

"That's when I knocked the ladder over and the window broke."

"*Right*!" Doc's eyes were alight with amusement. "How dumb do you think I am? You're not really a painter."

Stan shook his head. "No."

"FBI or CIA?"

He grinned. "NSA."

"Figures," Doc mused with a shake of his head. "I noticed you favored your right leg some. How long have you been out of rehab?"

Stan shifted his weight. "Four months."

Several seconds of strained silence went by before Doc spoke again.

"Are you going to protect this little lady?"

"Yes, sir." Stan put his arm around her shoulders. "With my life."

Doc stuck his hand out. "That's all I need to know."

Stan shook it. "If you will excuse me, I better get the window covered before it gets too dark to see."

He went into the barn and she heard him rummaging around. A few minutes later, Stan came out with an armload of boards and headed back to the house.

Khamiel stood staring at Doc with her arms crossed and her toe tapping the ground.

"It's been a long day," Doc sighed. "Did you want to see me?"

"You old goat. Why didn't you tell me Number Ten was getting ready to lamb?"

He gave her a lopsided grin. “I thought you’d had enough surprises for one day.”

Her anger subsided and she realized they both had had a long hard day. “Doc, you look like you’re ready to drop where you stand. I want you to come up to the house and get some sleep.”

“I don’t want to put you out, dear.” He lifted his hand and brushed the side of her face. “I’ll be fine here in the barn.”

“I won’t hear of it,” she argued. “I know you and Mother were more than just friends, and I won’t need her bed after all.”

Stan set the boards down outside and went into the kitchen for a drink. The telephone rang.

He sat his glass of water down and picked up the receiver. “Hello.”

“Who’s this?” a man asked.

“I’m the painter. Who’s this?”

He carried the handset into the master bedroom and opened the secretary. His fingers flew across the keyboard.

“Never mind who this is. I need to speak with Khamiel.”

“She isn’t here,” he lied. “She had to go to Atlanta.”

Stan heard a muffled conversation in the background. “I don’t believe you. She wouldn’t run off and leave a stranger there all alone.”

“Listen, pal, I don’t care if you believe me or not,” Stan growled. “If you want to talk to her, you can call back on Saturday.”

"That may be too late." He paused. "Tell her Leon is in trouble and she's the only one who can help. She has the number."

"What kind of trouble?" Stan asked trying to stall Leon. "Is he in a hospital?"

"No, she has something I need."

"What is it?" Stan asked. "I'll pass the information on to her."

"I'm not about to tell you." The voice increased in volume and irritability. "Have her call immediately. It's a matter of life and death."

"Wow, that sounds pretty serious." Stan smiled.

"Damn right, it's serious."

"I still think you should tell me so I can pass it on to her."

"I ain't telling you jack-shit, mister."

"I'll tell her what you said, but I can't promise she'll return your call, Leon."

"Just make damn sure you do."

The phone went dead.

"Stan?" Khamiel called out from the direction of the kitchen.

"I'm in here."

"I convinced Doc he needed a good nights' rest." She came into the room. "I gave him mother's bed."

He stared at the computer screen. "Did Leon say where he was going?"

"No, I just assumed it was back to California." She moved to stand beside him. "Did he call?"

"Yes. I was able to get a partial trace before he hung up." He tapped the screen with his index finger. "The son-of-a-bitch is still in Atlanta."

"Did he say why he called?" Khamiel paced across the room.

"He said you have something he needs."

"Well," she huffed. "It's not my pussy, he can charm his way into almost any panty he sees. Hell, he's had half the women in the bureau and the rest are on a waiting list."

"Which leaves us with..."

"*Chameleon!*" She stopped in the middle of the room and spun around. "The bastard's dirty."

Stan heaved a heavy sigh. "Apparently so. I'm sorry."

"Not half as sorry as he's going to be once I get my hands on him." She stormed out of the room, came back, and grabbed the phone.

Khamiel punched the numbers and waited.

"Go to *hell*!" She turned the phone off and set it on the secretary.

"Feel better?" He arched an eyebrow.

"Yeah, I do."

"Good, now call him back and apologize." He picked up the phone and held it out to her.

Her jaw dropped and her eyes widened. "I don't think I heard you. You want me to call the bastard up and...and..."

"Apologize."

"Why—in—the—hell should I?"

"Simple field tactics. We use him to lead us to the others." He held the phone by the antenna and let it swing back and forth. "I don't care what you have to promise him, just get him back."

"You're going to use me as bait." She snatched the phone from his fingers.

"Nothing personal, Khamiel. If I'm correct about who's behind this...I'd use my own mother."

"Okay..." she took a deep breath, "...let's do it."

Stan winked. "Give me a few minutes to set everything up."

Khamiel looked at the phone with nervous doubt and dialed Leon's number.

"Hello, Leon." *I think I'm going to be sick.* "I'm sorry I yelled at you. Please, forgive me."

"What's going on, Sugar Bear? Who's the creep who answered the phone?"

"Oh, sweetie..." She opened her mouth, stuck her tongue out and pointed her finger toward her throat.

Stan gave her a thumb up, grinned and watched the information print out across the computer screen.

"...you wouldn't believe the day I've had. CDC showed up and put the place in quarantine for two weeks and then this bumbling ass of a painter shows up and I'm stuck with him until it's over."

"Me," Stan mouthed the words, "a bumbling ass? Thanks a lot."

"Leon, dear, you need to check into a hospital and be monitored for the bird flu."

"I can't, Khamiel. I'm back in Los Angeles. That's why I called, I need your help."

"I don't know what I can do stuck out here in the middle of nowhere for two weeks, but I'll try."

"You don't have to go anywhere. You're sitting on what I need."

Leon sounded overconfident, sure of himself.

"What am I supposed to do, take a picture of my ass and send it to you? You're the one who ran out of here like he had his dick caught in the wrong cookie jar."

"That's why you're stuck in a desk job at Langley, Khamiel. You're not smart enough to be a field agent. I need information from your mother's computer."

That will be a cold day in hell. She flipped her middle finger at the phone.

Stan's shoulders shook as he silently laughed.

He grabbed a pen and paper and wrote, *You're doing great. We have a fix. Try to keep him on the line for a few more minutes. Agents are moving in as you speak.*

"Gee, Leon, I don't know if I can. All of Mother's lab files are password protected."

"All I'm interested in is the Chameleon file. If you don't think you're capable of figuring out the password, I can find someone who is."

Khamiel gritted her teeth.

"Be nice," Stan whispered.

She stuck her tongue out at Stan. "That was just a pipe dream of Mother's."

"The file exists, trust me."

"I'll see if I can find it."

"Call me back as soon as you do."

The phone went dead and she turned it off.

Stan jumped up out of the chair, grabbed her and spun her around. "You were brilliant." He gave her a huge kiss.

"Thanks." She pulled away, went into the bathroom and turned the shower on.

"Want me to join you?"

"No." She pulled her top over her head, "I'm going to bed. If you're hungry, there's food in the fridge."

She removed the rest of her clothes and stepped into the shower.

Leon's right, I'm not cut out to be a field agent. She poured a liberal squeeze of lavender body wash on a pink loofa and scrubbed. Steam boiled up around her in a thick cloud.

I should have known better. She scrubbed harder. *Damn him and damn me for getting involved with him.*

She dropped the loofa and leaned against the shower wall. *This is all my fault.*

"Khamiel?"

"Go away, Stan. Leave me alone." She slowly lifted her hand and turned off the water.

"I just wanted to say, this isn't your fault."

The bathroom door closed with an ominous metallic click.

Stan went into the kitchen and fixed a sandwich.

Doc came in and poured himself a glass of tea. "Where's Khamiel?"

"In bed." He took a large bite of his food.

"With the day she's had—" Doc took a sip, —"she needs the rest."

"You look like you could use some yourself, Doc."

The older man exhaled a long slow breath. His shoulders slumped. “It’s been a difficult week for everyone.”

“Tell me about her mother.”

Stan watched Doc’s face soften and his eyes mist over with unshed tears.

“Marie was a self-sacrificing woman, passionate about her work and dedicated to the study of science. In a word, she was brilliant. One of the top five scientific minds in the country, maybe even the world.”

Stan pondered Doc’s words. “Yet, she lived out here without a neighbor for miles around.”

“That was the other side of Marie.” Doc grinned. “Reclusive, a loner, she loathed any public recognition and, in the end, paranoid that her work would fall into the wrong hands.”

“You loved her,” Stan guessed. “Why didn’t you two ever marry?”

“I wanted to, after my wife died.” Doc’s face saddened with regret. “But Marie was already married to her work. I learned to be happy with what she was willing to give.”

Doc shook his head. “Enough of the past, I noticed the boards outside the door. Do you need some help with the window? I must warn you, I’m not much of a carpenter.”

“Damn, I forgot all about it.” Stan finished his sandwich in two bites. “You can hold the light for me.”

Doc sat his empty glass in the sink. “That I can do.”

Chapter Seven

Stan woke with an alarm bell going off inside his head. Only thing was, his eyes were open and he could still hear it. He grabbed his pants and stumbled into them on his way to the kitchen. “What is it, Max?”

“We have an emergency in the lab. Better put the water on to boil.”

“Turn off the alarm, Max.” Stan bolted for the elevator. “No need to wake the entire house.”

Stan reached the pen and felt helpless. “I need to know what’s going on.”

“I’m showing two new heat sources in the pen. One doesn’t seem to be moving. I’ll switch to infrared and put it on the monitor.”

“Damn.” He vaulted over the railing.

Using the monitor as a guide, he crossed the pen, dropped to his knees and found the still warm body of the lifeless lamb. With a quick swipe of his finger, he cleared its mouth and gently blew air into the tiny lungs.

Another quick glance at the monitor showed the ewe and the other lamb on the far side of the pen. “You may have given up on this one, but I haven’t.”

Stan gave the lamb several more short breaths of air.

"Come on, little one." He grabbed the lamb by its back legs, stood and swung it several times around in a circle.

Baaa!

He hugged the newborn to his chest. "I knew you could do it. Now we just have to convince mommy to let you eat."

The task proved easier said than done as he pitted his will against the elusive and uncooperative ewe. Stan sat in the middle of the pen and panted for breath.

"Max, is there any rope down here?"

"None is listed in my data banks. Why?"

"I'm going to tie up Number Ten so she can't run away from the other lamb."

"That would require you to catch Number Ten first. Something you seem incapable of doing."

"That's an astute observation, Max, but I didn't see you trying to help."

"I'm programmed to be observant, not to catch sheep."

Stan got up, brushed the straw from his jeans and left the pen.

"I detect a high level of hostility. Where are you going, Agent Freeman?"

"I'm going to find a substitute sheep." He picked up an empty beaker from a shelf and headed for the elevator.

"There are no other sheep around here."

He stepped into the elevator and entered his access code.

Nothing happened and he started to reenter the code.

"I must insist you return to the lamb. It will die without food."

Frustration tightened his voice. "Max, I need the milk out of the refrigerator, but I can't get it if the elevator doesn't move."

"Take the lamb with you."

"Oh, all right." He ran back to the pen. *Just what I need right now, a computer with PMS.* "I'll take it with me if it makes you happy."

"Thank you, Agent Freeman."

Stan wrapped the baby lamb up in a lab coat, ran back to the elevator and it shot up to the ground level.

"Nipple," he mumbled. "Got to have a nipple."

He rummaged through a cabinet and pulled out a pair of rubber gloves. "Mmm, this should work."

Stan filled the beaker with milk and set it on the stove to heat. He fashioned a nipple from the finger of a glove and wire tied it to the mouth of the beaker. "What do you think? I know it doesn't look like much, but it should work."

Baa!

Khamiel woke, stretched and looked around for Stan. She got out of bed and paused as she remembered why she had slept in her robe. It had worked. He hadn't even tried to kiss her good night. So why did she feel regret?

She went into the kitchen and came to an abrupt stop.

Stan sat on the floor fast asleep with his back against the elevator door. A beaker of milk lay on the floor beside him.

Her eyes narrowed. She cautiously approached and reached for the glass container.

Baa!

Khamiel jumped back and crashed into the table.

Stan's eyes fluttered open and he smiled. "Morning, you missed all the fun."

"So I see." She got down on her knees and lifted her hand. Her fingers found the wooly little head and she laughed. "It's so tiny."

"This one almost didn't make it." Stan picked up the bottle and placed it where he thought the baby lamb's mouth should be.

Instantly, he felt a hard tug on the bottle and hurried sucking sounds came from near his lap.

"It's hungry." Khamiel smiled.

"You should smile like that more often," he whispered. "It unlocks the beauty of your face."

Confused by his compliment, she stood and went over to the sink. "I'll put the coffee on before Doc gets up and decides to brew up some of his Café du Monde."

"Thanks, I'd appreciate it. It's been a long night."

Doc came into the kitchen wearing a pair of boxer shorts covered with bright pink bunnies. "Doesn't anyone sleep around this house anymore?"

"Good morning, Doc." Khamiel turned away and giggled. "Love your PJ's"

"When you get my age, you can wear any damn thing you want and to hell with what everyone else thinks, especially when they badmouth my coffee.

Doc yawned and stared at Stan. "Morning, Stan, you play wet nurse all night?"

Stan shifted his position on the floor. "Most of it. Mother rejected this one. The other one's doing fine."

"Other one!" Khamiel spun around. "You mean there are *two*?"

"Unless she has had another one since I came up here."

Doc grinned. "That would make three."

"Max!"

"I detect no new life forms in the pen."

She caught a collaborating wink between Doc and Stan.

"That will be about enough out of you two. I'll trade you both in for one good sheep dog."

Baa!

"See, even it agrees with me. Give me the damn thing before it breaks its neck trying to suck." As she knelt down and gingerly picked up the squirming bundle, she gave Stan a seething glare. "I thought you had experience with lambs?"

"Hey, don't get your panties in a bind," he protested. "I saved its life."

"Come on, little fella." She nuzzled the soft wool. "Let's find you a nice warm towel, preferably not a plaid." She carried the lamb down the hall.

Doc chuckled. "I guess it's up to me to make the coffee."

"I'll get it, Doc." Stan jumped to his feet. "You go ahead and get dressed." He winced as a thousand needles sent pain through his feet. A white-hot spear tore its way across his hip and down his leg.

"I don't think sitting on a hard floor all night was a very smart idea." Doc gave him a stern glare. "If you were my patient, you'd still have your ass behind a desk."

"No." Stan limped to the counter. "If I were your patient, my ass would be on a cold stone slab."

"Do us both a favor." Doc looked over the top of his glasses. "Make sure you don't end up there through all this."

"I don't intend for that to happen anytime soon. So, save the lecture until it does."

"Humph," Doc snorted as he left the kitchen. "Max isn't the only one around here with an attitude. Must be the coffee."

Stan waited as his morning caffeine fix slowly filled the pot.

His body screamed for a fix of a different kind, but he was determined to kick the pills, just as he had the needles. It was either that, or as Doc said, sit behind a desk for the rest of his life.

The final gurgle of water sounded. He filled a cup, lifted it to his mouth and inhaled the rich aroma. "Ahh."

Baa! Baa!

"Damn it! Come back here, you little shit."

He heard the stampede of tiny cloven hooves coming down the hall.

"Lamb on the loose," Khamiel warned in an agitated voice. "Everyone be careful where you step."

Stan shook his head and took a hesitant sip from the steaming cup.

The lamb entered the kitchen in a blur of colors as the wool tried to catch up with the speed of the lamb. It ran head first into Stan's legs and then squeezed itself between them and the counter.

"Here, lammie. Here, lammie, lammie, lammie." Khamiel crawled into the kitchen on her hands and knees, pausing every foot or so to reach out blindly around her. "Here, lammie, lammie."

Her gaping robe gave Stan a view that brought an instant stirring of his groin.

She lifted her head. “Have you seen lammie?” Her eyes closed and she scrunched her face. “Forget I said that, of course you haven’t seen the little shit.”

“Lammie is between my legs,” he replied with tongue in cheek.

Khamiel frowned. “That’s not the lammie I’m looking for, besides that one appears to be full grown.”

Stan took a step toward her and slowly squatted down. He tried like hell to keep from showing pain.

Concern flashed in her eyes. “Your hip?”

“I’ll survive.” He reached behind him and gently lifted the lamb off the floor.

“Lammie, come to mommy, you little stinker.” She took the newborn from his hands and hugged it to her breast.

“Thanks, I knew it was in here somewhere.” Suddenly, her mouth opened in a silent scream and her eyes nearly popped out of her head.

“Take it,” she screeched in a harsh panicked voice as she tried to pull the lamb away from her nipple. “The damn thing has teeth.”

Stan fell backward, slid down the counter and rolled onto the floor. “That’s gotta hurt.” Tears blurred his vision.

Baaaaa! The lamb voiced its complaint over not getting any milk.

Khamiel quickly pulled it away from her breast and thrust it into his hands.

“Want me to kiss it and make it better?”

“Don’t even think about coming near this breast.” She pulled her robe tight around her and secured the belt.

Stan petted the animal and it latched onto his finger. “He sure is a hungry little critter.”

"We have a slight problem." She stood, opened the refrigerator door and pulled out the almost empty milk jug.

"Do you have any powered milk?"

"What do I look like, a grocery store?" She set the milk on the table.

He sat the lamb on the floor and using the counter for leverage, pulled himself to his feet. "I guess I better call out the Calvary."

She frowned as she watched his slow movements. "I thought you said you were cleared for full duty?"

"So, I lied to the doctor."

"Anything I can do to help, Stan?" She reached out and touched his arm.

"Other than more damn pills when it's like this, a deep muscle massage is about the only thing that brings relief."

"You get the milk here and I'll massage anything you want."

"Well, in that case," he wiggled his eyebrows. "Break out the oil, the milk is on the way."

"Have you caught the damn thing yet?" Doc yelled from behind his closed door. "Sometime today would be nice."

"Just a minute, Doc." Khamiel put her hand close to the floor and wiggled her fingers. The lamb came to her and she held it with both hands. "Okay, Doc. It's safe to come out now."

"This place is turning into a zoo." He made a bee-line for the door. "I'll be back later."

Stan went in his room, pulled out his backpack and dug around for the secure phone.

Inside the NSA, the Special Projects Division existed as an enigma. There wasn't an office you could visit or a phone number you could call. Somehow, in a time when secret programs became tomorrow's headline news, it had remained under the radar of public scrutiny.

Those within the division were hand picked individuals from within the military and civilian population. They were the elite known as Omega Sentry.

As Field Commander, Stan had just two bosses: Omega Director, Scott Mathis and the President of the United States.

He hit the speed dial and it was answered on the first ring.

"Special Ops, Mathis speaking."

"Scott, how are you doing?"

"I'm doing better, but my physician says it's time to retire. My heart can't stand the stress anymore."

"Damn, sorry to hear that." Stan frowned. "How's Aleecia handling all this?"

"She's worried about me of course, but she's still going strong and young as ever. Must be all that seawater." Scott Mathis chuckled. "She and Angela are out swimming now."

"Is Scott Jr. around? I need him to run an emergency priority errand."

"As long as it's job related. I just chewed his ass for taking his new toy for a joy ride."

"It is. I need four big boxes of powered milk, two baby lamb bottles and nipples. While you're at it, send me a box of surveillance cameras. I'll leave the GPS on."

He heard his boss laughing. "Okay, I have it down. It may take some time to find everything. I think we're all out of baby bottles."

"Yeah, I figured it would. Appreciate it if you light a fire under this. I have a little one here that is getting pretty vocal."

"I'll get right on it. Now, you listen to me, Stan. I just got off the phone with the president. This comes straight from her—*no* heroics. The FBI has Haufmyer under surveillance. Alpha and Bravo teams are at Dobbins Air Force Base awaiting further orders."

Stan felt a persistent nudge against his pant leg.

"Thanks, Scott. Hopefully we won't need them. I've got to go."

"Good luck."

The phone went dead.

Stan reached down and picked up the lamb. "What are you doing back here?"

"It followed you." Khamiel leaned against the doorjamb. "How soon 'til the milk arrives?"

Baa! Baa!

"According to this one, it should have been here by now." The lamb tried to suck on his ear." Oh no, you don't. I think it's time for you to go back down with the others."

"I was thinking of putting a ribbon and maybe a bell around their necks." Khamiel crossed the room and petted the lamb. "It would help locate them easier."

"Good idea." He stepped around Khamiel, put the lamb in the bathroom and closed the door. "You find the ribbon and I'll wait for the milk to arrive."

"Should be some in the Christmas boxes." She walked over, gave him a quick kiss and brushed her fingers across the front of his jeans. "I hope the milk gets here soon."

"I'm—sure it will." He picked the phone up and went back to the kitchen.

Twenty minutes later, Khamiel came in. "What! No milk yet?" She held a red and blue ribbon, each with its own small bell attached.

"*No,*" he growled as his fingers tapped a staccato drum roll on the table.

His phone rang. Stan picked it up. "Hello."

"Special delivery arriving out back in two minutes."

He turned the phone off. "It's here."

"I'll run down to the road and get it."

He grinned. "It's not coming by car." He got up from the table. "Come on."

Khamiel followed him behind the house. "Why are we back here?"

Suddenly a high-pitched pulsating whine filled the air. They looked up to see a miniaturized version of a stealth fighter slowly descend and gently touch the ground.

Stan waved and ran over as the cockpit opened. "Your dad said you had a new toy. How's it handle?"

Scott Mathis Junior's smile filled his helmet visor. "Like a dream, but acceleration is a bitch. I can fart over Boston and be in St. Louis before you could smell it."

Stan laughed. "You got everything I ordered?"

"Yeah, it's down below." A long slim door opened in the underbelly of the jet.

He released the holding straps, grabbed the package and hurried away from the aircraft. Stan turned around once he reached Khamiel's side and gave Scott a salute.

The aircraft lifted straight up into the air, stopped and like a bolt of lightening, shot out of sight.

"Wow!" Khamiel stared up at the sky where only a thin vapor trail remained. "What was that?"

"That, my dear, doesn't exist...officially." He put his arm around her shoulder. "Just like what you have in the lab doesn't exist."

"I think I'm in over my head."

"You've been from the moment you came home." Stan gave her a reassuring squeeze. "That's why I'm here.

"Come on..." he gave her a slight tug, "...we have a hungry lamb to feed."

"And I have a massage to give."

Chapter Eight

"Where would I hide...if I were a bottle of massage oil?"

In someone else's house, I'd be in the nightstand—but this is my mother's house. "So the last place I would look, would be..." Khamiel pulled out the nightstand drawer.

At one time or another, when working around crime scenes and evidence, one comes across various pleasure enhancers and erotic sex toys. Finding them in your mother's nightstand was—akin to when you realized your parent's still had sex, and they were over forty.

"Did you find anything?" Stan asked from the doorway.

Khamiel felt her face flush as she slammed the drawer closed and looked around the room...didn't matter at what just as long as it wasn't in his direction. "Yes."

"Good." He breathed a sigh. "I've fed the lamb and I put the red ribbon around his neck. I'm going to our bed and lie down."

"I'll be there in a minute." *Our bed...hmm...I think I could get used to that idea.*

She opened the drawer, reached in and pulled out the first bottle she could find that didn't require touching any of Mother's toys.

Khamiel closed the drawer and looked at the label. "I hope, you like strawberries."

"To eat?" His voice sounded tired, muffled.

Khamiel looked at the bottle, covered her face with her fingers and giggled. "I suppose you could eat this if you wanted to, it says it's edible."

Stan lay naked, face down on the bed. The muscles in his right leg quivered. "Next time I decide to sleep sitting up on the floor again—do me a favor. Give me a swift kick in the pants."

"What were you expecting when you got off the injured list—" she crossed the room and climbed up on the bed, "—a nice cushy resort with room service, warm beaches, and exotic women in skimpy bikinis?"

"Not exactly—I prefer the topless beaches."

Khamiel slapped the left cheek of his firm bare ass.

Stan chuckled.

She applied the oil to his leg and began to rub it in—careful not to cause him any further pain. The room filled with the decadent fragrance of warm strawberries.

"You're going to have to massage harder if you want to do any good. Use your thumbs to get deep into the muscle."

She worked her way up each quivering roll of taut flesh in his right leg and hip. Stan turned his face away from her, and other than an occasional low groan, never made a sound. Ever so slowly, his muscles began to loosen and relax.

"I've done about all I can do here, let's have the other side."

Stan rolled over and flopped his arm across his eyes. "You have good hands."

"Thanks."

Khamiel started at the knee. About mid-thigh, she hit a muscle that felt like a roll of salami had been implanted under the skin. She worked her thumb around and into the muscle.

His upper body recoiled off the bed. His heaving chest and wild eyes gave her insight as to the pain's intensity.

Khamiel grasped his shoulders and leaned her head against his. "I'm sorry," she whispered.

"Don't worry about it." He lay back on the bed.

His thin-lipped smile did little to lessen her guilt.

"You caught me off guard."

She moved her hands up his thigh. As she tortured the muscle into submission—another became harder.

Her fingertips brushed against his balls. His steady deep breathing faltered and his stomach muscles tightened. Beneath her fingers, she felt the pulse beat of his femoral artery kick into overdrive.

His beautiful cock stood proud and tall from within its bed of curly blond hair.

Khamiel longed to touch him, taste him—feel him deep inside her, but not just yet. She poured more lotion into her hands, switched legs and started over. "You need to learn how to relax. You're way too tense."

Stan moved his arm and lifted his head from the pillow. The color of his eyes had deepened to a passionate dark turquoise. His gaze fueled the heat between her legs and her inner desire.

Her fingers trembled in anticipation as she untied her robe.

His eyes widened at the sight of her naked flesh. He lifted his hand and lightly brushed his fingers down her neck and over her breast.

She leaned forward wanting—needing more than just a tender caress.

Stan touched her hard nipple and rolled it between his thumb and finger.

"Oh!" she moaned. "Yes!"

He started to move his hand away. She grabbed his wrist. "*More.*"

She grasped his cock and ran her fingers over its wet silky smooth head. His fingers tightened around her nipple. "Ahh," she moaned.

His other hand pushed between her legs and he rubbed his finger along the sensitive lips of her vagina.

"You're wet," he whispered in a harsh passion-strained voice.

She couldn't speak as every nerve ending, every muscle, stood poised ready to catapult her off the edge of a high cliff.

He slipped a finger inside her and his thumb massaged her clitoris.

Spasms rocked her body in climatic release.

"That isn't fair," he chided her.

"Sure it is." She lowered her head and kissed his lips. Her hand slowly stroked the length of his hard shaft. "I'm allowed more than one at a time."

Khamiel placed soft, feather-light kisses on his chin, down his neck and across his broad chest. She sucked the hard flesh of his male nipple and gently nipped him with her teeth before moving lower.

She felt his low animal-like growl rumble deep in his chest. Khamiel lifted her eyes, smiled and then turned her head. Snake-like, her tongue darted from between her lips to taste and tease the musk covered tip of his cock. "Yummy, just a hint of strawberry."

Stan clasped his hands around her waist, pulled and rolled. He straddled her hips, grabbed the bottle of lotion and removed the top. "My turn."

Khamiel laughed, wrapped her fingers around his hand and twisted. “I don’t think so.”

Pink lotion erupted from the bottle and landed in a thick glob between her breasts.

“That’s cold!” She continued her struggle to wrestle the bottle from his hand.

He lost his balance and landed on top of her with the bottle between them. More lotion spewed out.

Stan got the bottle away from her and set it out of reach. He tried to sit up but she latched onto his arm, pulled and he fell off to the side.

Khamiel threw her legs across his hips and climbed on top.

He smeared the lotion across her breasts, stomach and on her legs. Then Stan grasped her behind the knees and pulled.

She twisted and turned within his slippery hands. Her hot, wet pussy landed in his face.

“Mmm.” He licked her clitoris. “You’re right, this strawberry is good.”

She wiggled her hips. “Didn’t your mother teach you any manners? *Ahh! Yaw lot oposed ew alk wa yaw mouf fuw.*”

“Sorry,” he laughed as he licked her hot flesh, “I didn’t understand a word you said.’

She removed her lips from around his cock. “I said, ‘You’re not supposed to talk with your mouth full’.”

He blew a raspberry against her clitoris.

“Hey!” She spun around on his slippery stomach. “I’m the one who’s supposed to be giving the blowjob.”

“There are times...” he pulled her head down and kissed her, “...when you talk too much.”

"Oh, really?" She sat up and crossed her arms under her breasts. "And just what do you intend to do about it?"

"This!" In one fluid motion, he sat up, clasped his hands around her waist and twisted. She landed on her back with her legs spread. Stan kissed her open mouth as he buried his hard cock inside her.

Khamiel lifted her hips and locked her legs behind his ass. "*Oooahhh*," she moaned.

Their tongues touched and darted back and forth. Her hungry kisses grew wild, more demanding. Fingernails dug into his back and raked his skin.

Her hips ground into his with each hard thrust. Her eyes swirled with a fathomless, black ardent desire. Her moans grew with passionate intensity. "*Ahh...yes—oh yes*!"

Just when he thought it impossible to hold on another second, Khamiel arched her back. She clamped her legs tighter around him. "*Ahh!*"

Stan felt the raw animal power of her climax. It enveloped him in an erotic euphoria of satisfaction. His body shook as he plunged into her wet silky depths and plummeted with her into ecstasy.

He rolled onto the bed beside her and pulled her close. "Oh *wow*," he panted.

"*Mmm*," she murmured in his ear, "I agree."

"Good thing I didn't get massages like that in rehab." His fingers toyed with her long black hair.

Khamiel breathed softly against his ear. "Why's that?"

"I'd never have left." Stan kissed the side of her face. *Then, I'd never have met you.*

The thought sobered Stan like a bucket of ice water.

"Are you okay?" She leaned up and propped her weight on her elbow. "You just shivered."

He smiled and kissed her. "I couldn't be better."

Stan swung his legs off the bed and reached for his jeans. "Thanks for the massage."

Khamiel sat up. "Where are you going?"

"I have a house to paint." He leaned over and trailed the back of his fingers down her cheek. "If Doc doesn't see me outside, he might wonder what I'm doing."

With a toss of her head, she laughed. "What makes you think I care what Doc thinks about us?"

Stan gave a long, thoughtful look at her face. When she laughed, sexy little dimples appeared in her cheeks and the laugh lines at the corner of her mouth were always there, ready to brighten her smile like a burst of sunshine on a cloudy day. But it was the twinkle in her eyes that convinced his heart and mind of the truth. *It's not my place to tell her.*

"Maybe you don't, but—" he lowered his head, tipped her chin up and softly kissed her lips, "—I do."

He picked up his shirt and put it on as he left the bedroom.

Khamiel opened her mouth to speak, and then, bewildered, she closed it and looked at her reflection in the dresser mirror. "What the hell just happened? I can't believe he walked out on me."

She scooted off the bed. "Of all the damn nerve." Khamiel went into the bathroom, turned around and walked back to the dresser. "One minute he was all lovey-dovey and the next he can't get away fast enough."

She paced back across the room. "Why the hell should he care what Doctor Davidson thinks? *I don't!*" She lifted her arms in the air. "Hell, he's acting like the odd man out in a sick love triangle. Surely, he doesn't think Doc and I are lovers."

Khamiel stopped in her tracks. The idea was so ludicrous, she laughed and continued pacing.

"Maybe it's a professional ethics problem and he's afraid Doc will report him," she mused. "There could be something in his records. Maybe he has a history of fraternization and if one more incident is reported he could face the discipline board and be court-martialed."

That didn't make sense either. What woman in her right mind would ever complain about his personal attention, on or off the job?

She remembered his comment about rehabilitation. "I bet one of the nurses came on to him and when he didn't return the affection, she complained. That has to be it. I'd like to find that little twit-nosed bitch. By the time I'm finished with her, she'll never touch another man, patient or otherwise."

Khamiel stopped pacing. "Damn it! Why wouldn't he tell me? I would've understood."

She went to the bathroom and stepped into the shower. "Instead, he treats me like a damn twenty-dollar street whore...*Slam—Bam*, he's done and out the door."

Her ire at a slow boil, Khamiel finished her shower, dressed and headed for the kitchen.

Doc Davidson sat at the kitchen table with an amused twinkle in his eye.

"Hi...Doc. Ah...how long have you been...here?"

"You mean sitting here at this table?" The corner of his lips twitched. "Oh, long enough, I guess." He tried to hide his smile behind a coffee cup. "Stan about knocked me over as I came through the door."

Khamiel felt her face flush. She whirled around, but fought the desire to run back to bed and cover her head with the pillow.

"I just came to tell you, I have to return to Atlanta and the CDC team is getting ready to leave too. They came up empty for a virus source. With no source, they can't justify keeping the place in quarantine. If you two start feeling sick, give me a call—immediately."

She pushed her thoughts on how to kill Stan out of her mind. Khamiel pulled out a chair and sat opposite Doctor Davidson. "If they couldn't find the virus source here, then where did my mother come in contact with it?"

"I'm sorry, Kamie. I wish I knew."

"You called me Kamie. Mother used to call me that when I was a little girl."

"I know." He reached over and placed his hand on hers. "She talked a lot about you. You were always her little Kamie."

"That was...a long time ago."

Doc sighed with longing, "Yes it was."

He got up, came around and placed a kiss on her head. "Call me if you need anything."

Chapter Nine

Khamiel Roche flinched as the kitchen door closed with a disheartening note of unresolved finality.

The source of her mother's killer, the H5N6 virus, remained a mystery, and would likely remain so. For with the passing of time—providing there were no new outbreaks of the deadly virus—Marie Roche; winner of the Nobel Peace Prize, dedicated scientist, and last of all...mother...would become just another sad statistic.

The answer had to be right in front of them, but why couldn't anyone see it? "Maybe we're not asking the right questions."

A big yellow smiley face popped up on the kitchen monitor. Its eyes shifted from side to side.

"Yes, Max."

"You said 'we', but I don't see anyone here with you. We implies more than one person."

"Max, I know the meaning of *we*. I included Doctor Davidson and the CDC team." She got up from the table. "Why am I arguing with a damn computer?"

"They have left, therefore should not be included in..."

Her fingers closed into a fist. Khamiel gritted her teeth. "Max!"

"My, my, aren't we agitated this morning."

"Max, run your system maintenance analysis program."

"There is no need to run the program at this time."

Khamiel went to the master terminal and manually selected the program. A message box popped up on the screen.

Do you wish to override scheduled maintenance?

"Yes."

Running this program will cause some programs not to function until it is finished.

"Continue."

Once started, aborting program may cause damage to system.

"Continue."

It is strongly recommended to run this program during low-use hours.

"Damn pop-up windows," she growled. "Continue."

Are you sure, you want to run system maintenance at this time?

"Yes!"

Nothing happened. Khamiel clenched her jaw, jabbed her finger on the mouse key and smiled as the screen went blank. "That should keep you busy."

She went to the elevator only to find the keypad dark and unresponsive. "Maybe I should have stayed in bed."

The phone rang. She whirled around and ripped the receiver from its cradle. "Hello!"

"Hello, Sugar Bear."

"Leon, what a surprise." Her voice dripped with sarcasm. She felt like barfing. "What the hell do you want?"

"Do you have the file I asked for?"

"No, Leon, I'm not giving you the file. Besides the computer's down."

"Listen, Bitch! As soon as you finish running the maintenance program, you better work on getting me the Chameleon file or a lot of innocent people are going to die—just like your mother. Oh, while you're at it, I want one of the lambs, too."

"What are you talking about, Leon?" Khamiel's eyes darted around the room. Her throat constricted and she had a burning lump in her chest. Sweat broke out on her palms.

"Don't play the dumb broad routine with me. I know everything that's going on, including your NSA friend and the surveillance team coming for my ass. What did you think I was going to do?" he snarled. "Sit in that flea-bag hotel and wait for them?"

"You better get used to small rooms, Leon. You're going to be in one for a long time."

"I have a million reasons for getting the Chameleon file, and neither you, your new fuck partner, or any of those blundering agents are going to stop me."

"Fuck you, Leon."

He laughed. "Wow! You finally got around to saying the word."

She heard a rustle of paper. "Oh! One more thing—do you remember Agent Skip Ebert from the Academy?" She could almost see the sneer on Leon's face.

"Yes...why?" she asked.

"You might want to call his wife. Let her know that, thanks to *you,* she's now a widow."

The phone went dead.

The receiver slipped from her fingers as she slowly sank to the floor.

Stan looked up and at that precise moment; gravity overcame a glob of paint's resistance to falling. It landed on his face below his left eye and ran down his cheek. He reached for his rag.

"Damn, it never fails." *I get on top of a ladder and realize I forgot something.*

He laid the paintbrush across the top of the can, got down and stomped off toward the kitchen. "I'm glad I don't do this for a living."

Stan opened the door.

Khamiel sat on the floor with knees drawn up to her chest and her back to the kitchen cabinet. Her arms were wrapped around her legs. Her eyes were red and swollen. She had a farway stare on her face.

He rushed to her side. "Khamiel..."

She lifted her left arm and placed her fingers on his lips. "Outside," she whispered.

He helped her up and put his arm around her waist. Khamiel leaned against him as he walked her outside. "What's going on?"

"Leon called. He shook the surveillance team." Her lips trembled and her eyes overflowed with tears, "I think an agent I went through the academy with is dead." Khamiel buried her face against his shoulder. "Skip was married and his wife recently had a new baby."

"I'll give the office a call and find out." He held her close. "Hopefully, Max was able to get a trace on the call."

"Can't," she shook her head, "I shut Max down for system maintenance just before Leon called.

"Stan, he knew about the computer being down, about the lambs and said more will die of the bird flu if I don't give him what he wants."

He stepped back, lifted her chin with his curled index finger and frowned. "You picked a hell of a time to shut Max down."

"I'm sorry. I was pissed at you, Doc told me he was going back to Atlanta and then Max started to annoy the hell out of me."

"Really?" He smiled and kissed her forehead. "I thought I was the only one he did that to."

"Afraid not." She laid her head back on his shoulder. "What are we going to do now?"

"Well, it's obvious Leon bugged the house when he was here, so first thing we do is find them. Then, we wait for him to make the next move."

"Hopefully, the bastard will make a mistake." Khamiel backed away and straightened her shoulders.

"I'm counting on it."

"You might want to start in the bathroom." She frowned as she got a good look at Stan. "You look like you got more paint on you than the house."

Almost immediately, he found a small round transmitter under the lip of the bathroom sink. Stan flushed it down the toilet. He filled the sink, soaked a washrag and scrubbed at the dried paint.

"Here, let me do that." Khamiel took the washrag from him. "The way you are scrubbing, you won't have any skin left."

The corners of her mouth turned up in a slight smile. Tiny laugh lines pointed to her cheeks where sexy dimples played peek-a-boo. Her eyes twinkled with dazzling sensuality.

It took considerably longer for her to take the paint off than it had for him to put it on.

Stan took the wet washrag from her fingers. “Before we get sidetracked and I end up making love to you on the bathroom floor, we have more transmitters to find.”

Khamiel put her arms around his neck, pressed against him and gave him a tongue-probing kiss. “If you insist.”

“What other rooms was Leon in while he was here?”

She thought for a minute and felt heat rising up her neck. “With the connecting door to the other bedroom, he could have been in all of them.”

“I found the one in here. Let’s get started on the other rooms.”

Three hours later, after crawling around on their hands and knees, looking under, inside and on top of every item in the house, they had three more small transmitters laid out before them on the kitchen table.

Stan turned two of them off.

“You know, Stan.” She stopped him from turning off the last transmitter. “I am so glad I met you.”

“Oh! Why’s that?”

“Now, that I’ve known what a real man is like in bed, I realize that I’d have had as much pleasure masturbating with a pencil as sleeping with Leon...maybe more.”

“Ouch,” Stan mouthed and then snickered. “You mean he’s a pencil-dick.”

"No, he's worse—Leon Haufmyer is a selfish *prick*. He doesn't care if he satisfies a woman or not, just as long as he gets off."

She got up, came around the table and sat on his lap. "Stan, if you had never walked again—" Khamiel wrapped her arms around his neck. "—you would still be twice the man as Leon."

Her lips met his in a tender, loving kiss.

She broke the kiss, picked up the third transmitter and turned it off. "That wasn't a jibe at Leon. Okay, maybe it was." Khamiel held up her thumb and index finger. "But just a little one. I meant every word."

"System Maintenance complete, all systems normal— just like I tried to tell you." Max came online with an infrared picture and audio of the sheep. The heat image of number Ten and Blue were merged together. Red Ribbon stood on the other side of the pen. He was apparently hungry and being very vocal about being neglected.

"I'll get the milk ready." She gave him a quick peck on the lips and scooted off his lap.

"I better call the office." As Stan reached for the phone, it rang.

He picked it up. "Scott, I was just about to call you."

She filled the bottle and stretched the nipple over its neck. "I'll be in the lab."

Red met her at the door and followed her over to a bale of hay. "Have you and Blue been playing?"

Another bell jingled as Blue came running over.

She held the bottle for Red as Blue nudged her leg. His little woolly head turned the same shade of brown as her slacks. "I bet you would look funny if I wore my tropical print."

Baa!

Blue decided he was still hungry and Red's bottle was a lot closer than mommy's teat. He head-butted Red away and made a grab for the bottle.

Khamiel picked her feet up. "Why do I have to be in the middle of this?"

"You make a pretty surrogate mother." Stan leaned on the top rail of the pen.

"I didn't hear you come in." She knew the look on his face. It wasn't good news.

He crossed the short distance between them and with a heavy sigh, sat beside her. "There's no easy way to say this...Agent Ebert was part of the surveillance team watching Leon. He was killed early this morning."

She picked Red up and put the animal in her lap. Her heart ached for Skip's wife and child. Leon didn't deserve a jail cell. He needed something a lot smaller.

"I'm sorry." Stan put his arm around her shoulders. "The agency will find him."

"They better find him before I do." She wiped her eyes.

Stan held the bottle up while the lamb drank.

Khamiel laid her head on his shoulder. "Do you think whoever is behind all this will release the virus?"

"I don't know." He kissed the top of her head. "Let's hope it doesn't come to that."

Red finished eating and seemed content lying in her lap. “Hey, don’t get too comfortable. You’re staying down here where you belong.”

Baa!

Stan laughed. “I think that was maaa-mmy.”

“Sounded more like daaa-ddy to me.” She put Red in his lap. “Don’t forget to tuck it in.”

He stood and carried the lamb over to the pen. “Fine, as long as I don’t have to sing a lullaby.”

Chapter Ten

"Good morning, Khamiel."

"I fail to see anything good about it."

"You are grouchy today. Did you get up on the wrong side of the bed? Maybe you need more sleep?"

She ignored Max, crossed the lab and went into the other room.

Baa! Baa!

The tinkling of bells at her feet brought a tired smile to her face. "Blue Ribbon," she scolded, "how many times do I have to tell you?" She plopped down on a bale of hay and pushed the lamb away. "This milk is for Red."

Red didn't need to be told twice. He latched onto the nipple and nearly jerked the bottle from her hand.

"Hey, slow down," she laughed. "There's more where this came from."

Baa! Baa!

"Oh, shut up, Ten." She flipped her hair from her face. "If you were doing your job, I wouldn't be down here in the middle of the damn night feeding your baby."

Baa!

"Yes, I can see you're out of hay. I'll get more as soon as I finish feeding Red."

Blue Ribbon jumped up on the hay bale with her and started chewing on her hair.

"You little pain in the ass," she said pushing it away. "Go find your mama's teat and leave me alone."

"I do not think they are old enough to understand English. There is no need to be harsh with them."

She glared up at the camera. "Max, I do not need you to tell me what to do, or not do, concerning these lambs."

"I watch over them, tell you when they are hungry and you treat me like this. Humph, that's gratitude for you."

A tuff of hay floated from the bale, and as it danced in the air, slowly began to disappear.

An extra hard tug on the nipple pulled the bottle from her hands. Khamiel lunged, but it went bouncing across the room. She sat on the floor, pulled her knees up to her chest and wrapped her arms around them.

"Damn." She blew her tousled hair from in front of her face.

Baa!

"Okay, Ten." She stood, her arms hung limp by her side. Her shoulders slumped. "I'll bring you a bale of hay."

She took the hay hook from the wall, stabbed a bale and dragged it to the gate. "Stand back, Ten. I'm too damn tired to toss this over the rail."

"Max, bring up infrared on the monitor, please."

"Max, I'm waiting," she clinched her jaw.

The overhead monitor finally changed. "Thank you, Max."

Ten stood on the far side of the pen. Khamiel unlatched the gate and swung it open just enough to get the bale through. She took her eyes off the monitor for a second.

Ten slammed into her side, pushed her against the railing and got free.

Khamiel kept one eye on the monitor as she ran after the fleeing ewe. “You can’t get out of here.” She stopped. Gasping for breath, she bent over and placed her hands on her knees.

Ten moved off to the left and as Khamiel turned her head to watch the monitor. The ewe bolted back toward the pen.

Damn, I forgot to close the door to the lab.

“No! Ten!”

Not to be left behind, Blue Ribbon followed its mother through the open door, with Red bringing up the rear.

“*Damn it!*” She exhaled a couple sharp breaths, shook her head and stood up straight. “I’m beginning to hate sheep.”

With determination in her stride, she marched into the lab. *Maybe I can use Blue to lure Ten and Red back into the other room.*

She picked up the milk bottle from where Red had dropped it, but the lambs were having too much fun exploring to pay her any attention. When she went left, then Blue would go right, and round and around the lab they went.

All of a sudden, Blue headed right for her. The ribbon around his neck bobbed and leapt into the air.

“You little shit, I’ve got you now.” She made a quick grab for it as it ran by and snagged a leg. “Back into the other room you go.”

Baaaaa! Baaaaa!

“That’s right, call for Mommy.” *This is going to be easier than I thought.*

A speeding wool covered truck slammed into her chest and shoved her backward into a table. She lost her balance, her hold on the lamb, and fell to the floor.

Glass crashed above her. Pain shot up her arm as a jagged shard pierced her hand. Thick dark green liquid flowed off the table, into her palm and...disappeared into the wound like water on a dry sponge.

Her hand turned ice cold and then exploded with an intense burning pain that crawled up her arm. She bit her lip against the agony. Large beads of sweat covered her skin as the pain spread across her chest.

Khamiel pulled herself to her feet. The room began to spin. The tabletop lay covered in broken glass. The refrigerator door stood wide open and several bottles had overturned. Lying in a pool of the thick green liquid, she could see a label. Her heart pounded with fear as she tried to focus on the one word printed in bold letters.

Chameleon

Oh! God! What have I done?

Khamiel tried to walk. Her legs felt like soft rubber. She clawed at a table for support as the lights in the lab dimmed.

"Stan!"

At the sound of the alarm, Stan bolted from the bed. "What the hell. Max!"

"Khamiel has had an accident in the lab."

The access door to the elevator wouldn't open and he pushed the knob. "Call an ambulance, Max. Now!" He pushed the knob again and again until the door opened.

He pounded the keys as he entered the access code. The elevator started to descend.

"I'm sorry, Agent Freeman, but an ambulance or a hospital won't be able to help her."

The elevator stopped and he rushed to Khamiel's side—each breath came in a rapid harsh wheezing—her body oozed sweat from every pore. He checked her heart rate and knew real fear for the second time in his life.

Khamiel began to shake. He tried to check her pupils but only the whites of her eyes showed. The shaking grew worse 'til every muscle in her body convulsed out of control.

"There has to be someone you can call," he pleaded.

"There is no antidote for the Chameleon formula."

"Oh, God!" Anguish tore through his soul. Tears flooded his eyes. "*No*! This can't be happening." Stan checked her pulse and noticed it had slowed, but not by much. He picked her up and carried her to the shower.

"Do not give her a shower. It could trigger the wrong response and actually kill her."

"But, she's burning up."

"Her temperature is 106, it will begin to slowly lower on its own, if..."

"If what, Max!"

"If she is going to live."

"How do you know this, Max? What do you base this on?"

"From the data in my files."

"I have to do something, Max." He cradled her to his chest and rocked her. Tears streamed down his face. "I'll go crazy waiting."

"You can boil some water."

"Will that help?"

"No, but it will give you something to do."

Stan closed his eyes in frustrated anger. "I'm going to take her up and put her to bed."

"A very good idea, Agent Freeman, but you must hook up a camera so I can keep track of her condition. May I suggest one of the new perimeter cameras you installed."

"Max, there is something that I can do." He carried her to the elevator, held her close and squeezed into the small confined space with her. It began to rise. He knew it took only seconds, but it seemed an eternity.

Stan kicked the door open and carried her to the bedroom where he removed her sweat-soaked clothes and covered her with a sheet. He grabbed the last remaining camera with one hand, the phone with the other and dialed.

"This is Agent Freeman, Project Chameleon is Code Blue! Repeat, Code Blue, Medical Emergency." He hung up the phone.

"Max, the camera is on. Do you have visual?"

"Yes, Agent Freeman, I have visual. Her vital signs remain elevated but steady, which is more than I can say for yours."

"Would it be all right if I bathed her with a damp cloth?"

"Yes, that would be fine."

Stan hurried to the bathroom, dampened a washcloth and returned to her side.

"Her temperature has dropped two tenths."

"Is that a good sign?

With a soft, gentle touch, he wiped the sweat from her face, neck and upper body.

Max remained silent.

"Damn it, Max, I asked you a question."

"I don't know."

"What do you mean you don't know?" he snarled.

"All the information in my files deal with sheep."

"You are one of the most advanced computer systems in the world," his fingers gripped the cloth in a tight fist, "start computing and give me something to go on."

"Agent Freeman, your body temperature increase and rapid heart rate indicates your blood pressure is extremely high. You must try to remain calm."

Stan turned back to the bed and continued rubbing her body with the damp cloth. "Hang in there, Khamiel. I'm right here with you. Help is on the way."

Time seemed to stand still. He felt helpless.

"Agent Freeman, I show two aircraft approaching low over the trees from the North."

"Thank you, Max. I'm expecting them.

"Khamiel, the Calvary has arrived. I'll be right back." He leaned over and kissed her forehead. "Please don't die, my love."

He replaced the sheet over her, ran through the house and stood waiting out back as the first transport helicopter touched down in the field. Its large twin rotors threw grass and dirt into the air. A short distant to the left, the second helicopter touched down.

Doors opened at the rear of each helicopter and twenty men, carrying large backpacks, ran for safety outside the whirling arc of the blades. Less than five minutes later, both helicopters were gone and eighteen men with their equipment had vanished into the surrounding forest.

Agent Chelae Brooke and a man approached the house. Tall and thin like her mother, but more mulatto in color thanks to her father Scott Mathis; Chelae walked sure and confident across the ankle deep grass of the field.

Thanks to her mother and Scott's wife, Aleecia, Chelae's training in the Martial Arts made her one of the deadliest women in the world, with or without a weapon in her hand.

"Agent Brooke, thanks for getting here so quick." He shook her hand. "Let's go inside."

"Field Perimeter is being set up at two hundred yards," Chelae spoke as they walked around the house. "A full medical team will be here within the hour. This is Doctor Housel."

Stan shook his hand. "I don't know what the hell you can do, but I'm damn glad to see you. There was an accident in the lab and some experimental formula got into her blood stream.

"I'll show you the computer terminal and take you back to see Khamiel. All the research was done on sheep so you'll need to familiarize yourself with the project before treating her."

"Any idea how much of the formula got into her system?"

Stan blinked the moisture from his eyes and shook his head. "No."

Dr. Housel placed his left hand on Stan's shoulder. "We'll do what we can for her."

"Thanks." He pressed his lips together. "I know you will." He watched Doctor Housel pull the sheet back and begin examining Khamiel's feverish body.

Agent Brooke appeared in his peripheral vision. "Appearances can be deceiving, but it appears to me that—maybe you are too close to this case."

"That's why you're here, Chelae. I need you to cover my ass until I get my head straight." He glanced up at the camera. "First, I've got to get you past Max's watchful eye.

"Max?" She looked down the hall. "Who is Max?

"Come with me." Stan took her into the master bedroom. "Have a seat."

"Agent Brooke, I'd like you to meet, Max. Max, this is Agent Chelae Brooke. Until Khamiel gets well, Agent Brooke will be taking charge of security. She will have full access to all spaces."

"Agent Freeman, I cannot comply with your request. Secure spaces are for authorized personnel only. Any attempt to compromise security will activate a total lockdown."

"Well, I tried." Stan leaned over and whispered in Chelae's ear. "Would you by any chance happen to have the Mathis Key with you?"

An eye blink later, she held an MP3 disk in the palm of her hand.

He took the disk and quickly slipped it into the computer.

"What have you done, Agent Freeman? I do not recognize this program. Initiating security lockdown in five seconds...four...three...two...one...

"Security lockdown—has been—terminated, Agent Freeman, you have full access and control."

"Thank you, Max."

With a sigh of relief, he removed the disk from the computer, "Remind me to thank your dad for this." Stan kissed the disk and handed it back to Chelae.

"Initiate security clearance for NSA Agent Chelae Brooke." He inserted her identification card into the reader.

"How's your mother doing?"

"Stephanie's fine but she's worried about dad's heart. She and Aleecia pamper him to no end."

"Agent Brooke, you must hold still."

"Max gets a little testy at times."

"I do not."

Doctor Housel came into the room. "Khamiel is holding her own, Agent Freeman. I'm not sure how. Most of her vitals are off the chart from anything I've ever seen. I need to try and understand what we're dealing with."

"Chelae, if you will give the good doctor your chair, we'll let him get down to work."

Chelae Brooke stood. "Its all yours, Doc. Good luck.

"I'm going out and check the perimeter. I'll be back in a few." Agent Brooke left the room.

Stan got Doc Housel into the system and left him with Max's assistance to scour through the thousands of pages covering Dr. Marie Roche's lifetime of research.

He went in to check on Khamiel, sat on the edge of the bed and laid his hand on her forehead. She was burning up with fever and there wasn't a damn thing he could do about it. His heart felt like it was being ripped apart. He leaned over and kissed her lips.

"I've got to go down to the lab," he whispered in her ear, "but I'll be right back."

He went into the kitchen, entered the elevator and descended to the lab.

"Infrared mode, Max."

The lab showed no other heat source than his. He went to the other room, closed the door behind him and searched the monitor. Ten and the two lambs were in the pen.

He closed the gate and rested his arms on the top rail.

Baa! Red Ribbon got up out of the hay and came over to him. *Baa!*

Stan reached down, picked Red up and buried his face in the lamb's soft wool.

Baa!

"Come on, little fella. How about we find you something to eat?"

Baa!

He carried Red into the lab, found the bottle and got back into the elevator. Red began to stir and kick his legs. His wooly little head smacked Stan in the chin.

"Okay, I get the message." The elevator stopped. Stan set the animal on the floor and opened the door.

Baa! Red bolted down the hall, spun around, made a beeline back to the kitchen and got between Stan's legs.

Agent Brooke sat at the table with her mouth open.

Stan laughed.

Doctor Housel peeked around the corner.

Stan bent down and picked up the lamb. "Come in, Doctor Housel, it's time you two met Red Ribbon. His mother wouldn't claim him, so we've been bottle feeding him and right now he's hungry."

"Here, Chelae." He thrust the lamb into her arms. "Hold Red while I get the milk ready.

"How the hell am I supposed to hold something I can't see?"

"I'm sure you will figure it out." He laughed and turned to begin mixing the powered milk.

"Warning! Aircraft approaching, it's going to hit the house. Impact in thirty seconds, evacuate immediately."

The house began to vibrate—dishes rattled in the cupboards—a coffee cup danced across the table. Agent Brooke grabbed the cup before it fell and looked at her watch. "Right on schedule."

Red Ribbon broke free and sped down the hall toward Khamiel's room.

They went outside in the predawn gray and watched as a Vertical Takeoff and Landing Cargo-141 or "VTLC-141" slowly touched down behind the house. The back of the plane opened up and a semi-tractor and trailer drove down the ramp. On the side of the trailer was a large red cross and the words, Emergency Mobile Trauma Unit.

Three men and two women came down the ramp. It closed behind them and they hurried toward the house.

"I'm Agent Freeman and this is my second in command, Agent Brooke."

A man stepped forward. He was barely five-foot tall, thick black hair with white showing like racing stripes above the temple. "I'm Dr. Rosenthal. These are my colleagues: Drs.' Tracy King, Sonya Lasovich, Lewis Xynath and Jess Hines."

"If you will follow me, please. Time is of the essence, so I'll let Dr. Housel give you a briefing inside of the patient's condition and what information, or lack thereof, that he has gleaned from studying the files for the last hour."

"What about Red?" Chelae whispered. "Where did the lamb go?"

"There's a good chance it's hiding in the bedroom." Stan allowed a slight grin to form on his lips. He led the others to the bedroom and knelt down outside the door.

Doc Housel turned back the covers.

A red ribbon with a bell attached sprang into the air, fell to the floor and floated between Dr. King's legs. "*Aaack*!"

"What the fuck was that?" Dr. Lasovich jumped back.

Red leapt from the floor and landed in Stan's arms. His little body quivered.

"This is a little lamb. We call him Red Ribbon, for obvious reasons. Its mother was injected some months back under controlled conditions with the Chameleon formula. Roughly..." he looked at his wristwatch, "...three hours ago, an unknown quantity of the formula accidentally found its way into Khamiel's blood stream." His voice broke. "Time is not on our side."

"Agent Freeman is correct," Doctor Housel continued. "We have maybe thirty hours at the most to reverse the effects of the Chameleon formula."

"Or what?" one of the men asked.

"Ms. Roche will either be dead, or she may become like this little lamb—Chameleon."

Chapter Eleven

Dr. Housel checked Khamiel's pulse. "We need to get Ms Roche into a controlled environment with unrestricted access to laboratory equipment."

"Max, will the cargo elevator handle the truck that is outside?"

The new members of the medical team looked around the room in confusion.

"Yes, it will, but I do not like giving access to the laboratory to strangers."

Stan ignored Max's complaint. "We'll move Khamiel to the medical emergency unit and everyone can ride down together."

"What are we waiting for?" Dr King asked. "Let's do it."

"Max, when I drive the truck onto the elevator lower it to the lab access tunnel."

"I don't like this idea."

"Max, I don't give a damn what you like or don't like," Stan snapped. "Just do it!"

Dr. Hines reached down and scooped Khamiel up in his arms. "Lead the way, Agent Freeman."

"Agent Brooke, have one of your men escort the driver to the nearest town with bus service. Secure transportation to where ever he or she wants to go."

She keyed the transmitter on her belt. “Viper Two, report to command center.”

Stan led the group outside and approached the driver. “You’re not needed here anymore. One of my men will take you to town and put you on a bus.”

“I’m supposed to stay with the vehicle at all times.” The driver, a woman of mixed Eastern descent in her early thirties, glared at him.

“Not this time.” Stan smiled. “I just changed your orders.”

“This truck is my responsibility. I *demand* that I be allowed to stay with it.”

He was surprised at her venomous response.

A man dressed in combat fatigues came running up to the truck. “You wanted to see me?”

“Use that vehicle over there and take this woman to the closest bus station. I don’t care where it’s going, just make damn sure she’s on the next bus.”

“You can’t do that,” the driver snarled.

He gritted his teeth. “Agent Brooke, remove this woman from the area, immediately.”

“Yes, sir.”

Dr. King came around the back of the trailer. “We’re ready when you are.”

Stan climbed into the cab, fumbled with the gears and the truck started to move. He pulled into the barn, set the brakes and the huge elevator started its descent.

“Viper One to Viper.” The voice on the radio boomed and Stan turned the volume down on his receiver.

“Driver was madder than hell, but she’s on her way to town.”

"Thank you, Viper One. Close the barn doors and keep a sharp lookout. Once I drop the trailer, I'll bring it back up." Stan twiddled his thumbs at the slow rate of descent. Small florescent lights, recessed into the concrete wall, cast weird moving shadows inside the truck cab.

The elevator stopped with a jarring thud.

"Finally—now comes the fun part." He shoved the gearshift into reverse and began the long, slow process of backing the trailer one hundred yards to the laboratory.

Even though the temperature in the tunnel was down right chilly, his palms started to sweat. The light at the end of the tunnel appeared a long way off.

He backed the trailer into the large storage area, jumped out and lowered the stationary support pads. With a hurried grunt, he released the locking collar and separated the air hoses. Stan climbed back into the cab, released the brake and roared up the tunnel. As the elevator started up, he breathed a nervous sigh of relief.

Agent Brooke stood waiting for him inside the barn. "Took you long enough," she complained.

He shut the motor off and stepped down from the cab. "You try backing one of these down a hundred yard tunnel in almost pitch blackness."

"You're going to leave it here?" she asked.

"Yeah, keep it out of sight." He started toward the house.

"From whom?" She looked around. "The squirrels or the raccoons?"

"Nope, it's those pesky armadillos." He kept a straight face. "They're vicious this time of year."

Chelae grinned. "I forgot about—"

A violent explosion knocked them to the ground. Stan rolled over in time too see what was left of the barn flying across the field as thick black smoke billowed into a mushrooming cloud overhead.

"Brooke," he barked. "Set Condition Delta Two at all posts, if anything moves in the woods, I want it dead. Contact, Viper Two, I don't want him taking any chances with his passenger. Order termination code, X-Ray Zulu." Stan ran toward the house. "I'll be in the lab."

The lab was, as he suspected, in a state of confusion. The doctors all started asking questions at once. Stan held up his hand. "Yes, there was an explosion, but you are safe, for now. It appears the tractor was rigged to blow a certain length of time after the driver left it, or after it was shut off. You are still here so I would say that the trailer itself is probably not wired."

"But you can't be sure?" Dr. Lasovich asked.

"I'm going to check the trailer now. I know you're scared, but please, keep working."

Stan inspected the trailer with a fine-toothed comb, afraid that at any moment, it might be their last. His shirt stuck to his back and he had to constantly dry his hands on his jeans. He came up with nothing. The trailer was clean.

"How's she doing, Doc?" Stan picked Khamiel's limp uninjured hand up and clasped it in both of his. *If I hadn't gotten so close to you, this might not have happened.*

Dr. Rosenthal sighed and started to change the bandage on her injured hand. "They're running blood and tissue samples now. We know its spreading through her body, but we don't know how fast."

The sheet moved. *Baa!*

Dr. Rosenthal laughed. "This little lamb missed his mommy."

He lifted the sheet.

Red Ribbon lay by her side.

"You know," Doc continued, "as soon as I put the animal next to Ms. Roche, her vital signs stabilized. Don't misunderstand me, she is still critical but at least now, her readings aren't bouncing around all over the chart. They're just—off the charts as we know them."

Agent Brooke approached with a grim, tight-lipped expression on her face. "Agent Freeman, I need to talk with you—in private."

"Do what you can for her, Doc."

Stan walked down the access tunnel with her. "What's up?"

"Viper Two is down."

His gut tightened. He took a couple of deep anger-controlling breaths. Stan's mind took him back in time.

Pain, knotted like a ball in his stomach. A continuous roll of thunder pounded in his ears. Hot thick blood obscured his vision. Fear choked off his air and he fought for each agonizing cordite-laden breath.

"We tracked his GPS to the bus station. I contacted the local Sheriff. They found him in the back seat of the mini-van—with a broken neck. There's no sign of the woman. I called the FBI."

In the final seconds of consciousness, he saw her mocking smile.

"Son-of-a-bitch." Stan exploded in a rage. "I don't believe this. I had the bitch within my reach and let her get away."

"You don't think she's—"

"Damn right, I do." He marched back down the tunnel. "The driver didn't look like her, but I'd stake my life that underneath the facade, it was Leian Wooso of Chinese Intelligence."

Agent Brooke ran to keep up with him. "How did she get past security and onto our plane?"

"How the hell do I know?" Stan hit the lab door without slowing down and it crashed into the wall. "All I know is the bitch was here. I let her get away *again*—and because of that, we've lost another agent."

"Where are you going?" She held the elevator door open.

"To call Mathis."

"You're too emotionally involved. You told me that yourself. Why don't you stay down here and I'll call him?"

"That's the problem. Because I allowed myself to become involved, I wasn't thinking clearly, making it my fault Viper Two is dead." He poked Chelae between her breasts. "I don't need you, or anyone else sugar coating my fucking mistakes to Mathis."

He ripped the door from her hand and started for the surface.

"*May I say something*?"

"You probably will anyway, Max."

"Have you considered what might have happened had you not sent the driver away, or you had left the truck in the tunnel?"

Stan rested his head against the elevator wall and closed his eyes.

"Everyone in the laboratory would have died."

"Viper Two is still dead."

"One dead instead of seven or eight, sounds like you made the right choice."

"I'd rather not have lost any." The elevator stopped and Stan opened the door.

"One doesn't always get what one wants. For example, I'd rather not be a computer."

"Well, you are a computer so get over it." Stan headed for the bedroom master terminal.

"You're in command—get over it."

"Easier said than done, Max." He sat at the terminal. "Bring up visual files on anyone who had access to the laboratory in the three years prior to Dr. Roche's death."

Stan picked up a pencil and twirled it in his fingers while he waited.

Marie Roche and Doc Davidson's pictures appeared on the screen.

"That's it?"

"Yes."

"Go back three more years."

The pencil snapped in two. The face of Leian Wooso filled the screen, but the name listed was Lei Woo. "So this is where you were hiding for three years."

"Would you like me to go back further?"

Stan glared at the monitor. "No." He threw the pieces of the broken pencil across the room. "I found what I was looking for."

He picked up the phone and dialed.

Agent Brooke paced across the lab floor.

With a seemingly impossible deadline before them, tension among the doctors ran tighter than a banjo string.

She stopped behind the blonde doctor and looked over her shoulder.

"Know what you're looking at?" the doctor asked.

"Not really." Chelae glanced down the long counter. "I'm sorry, could you please give me your name again."

"It's Lasovich, but you can call me Sonya."

"Sonya is a lot easier. If I tried your last name very fast, I'd end up tying my tongue in a knot."

Sonya smiled. "I'm from Scandinavia."

"Wish we could have met under different circumstances, Sonya. What are you looking for?

"I'm conducting DNA fingerprinting using hair samples I took from her hair brush and comparing them with new samples Dr. Rosenthal is taking every half hour. This information will tell us to what extent her DNA has changed since the accident and the rate of development."

Chelae glanced over to the tall athletic black hunk starring intently at a computer screen. "What is Dr. Hines working on?"

"He's lost in his own little world." Sonya glanced up and smiled. "He is using the Tandem Mass Spectrometer to further break down Khamiel's DNA into proteins and amino acids. They are then compared with known values."

"What does that give you?" Chelae noticed that Sonya never stopped or slowed down what she was doing.

"Without going any deeper than necessary, simply put—we are looking for the enzyme catalysts that accelerate the Chameleon formula. Plus, we are trying to isolate the transport proteins that allow the mutated molecules to pass through the cell membranes. Once that is accomplished, we might be able to synthesize a blocker to stop the process from activating."

"Sounds like a lot of work." Chelae leaned against the counter. "How long will it take?"

"Well..." Sonya paused her work, swiveled her chair to the side and looked up. A large tear hung tenaciously in the corner of her eye. "It takes big drug companies ten to twenty years to find a blocker for a simple virus—and the Chameleon formula is anything but simple."

Sonya blinked and turned back to the worktable. She quickly lifted her hand to her face and swiped the tear away.

"Thank you." Chelae laid her hand on the woman's shoulder. "Do the best you can."

Dr. Lasovich nodded and went back to work.

Agent Brooke crossed the aisle to where the vibrant redhead, Dr. King, sat at Max's terminal.

"Agent Freeman seemed rather upset when he left."

"Just a little." Chelae grinned.

A new page of text flashed on the monitor every fifteen seconds. Frequently, Dr. King would stop and highlight a paragraph or even an entire page.

"In case you are wondering, I read a thousand words a minute. When I find something that looks like it might help or be of interest, I send it over to Dr. Xynath who puts it all together, compares it to what we know of Ms. Roche's condition at any given moment, which will give us some direction to go—if there is one."

"Any hope at all?" she asked.

"With the information I've retrieved from the files, my first response would be no, but I've been wrong once before."

"I won't bother you any longer. Thanks."

She stood with her hands on her hips and took a long look around the lab. An air of frantic helplessness permeated the room. Yet, they worked on—feverishly fighting against a clock that they knew in their hearts, they couldn't beat.

She breathed a sigh of regret. Her vision blurred. Her lips trembled. Chelae turned away and rubbed her eyes.

"How are you holding up?"

She turned to see Dr. Housel standing next to her.

"I'm managing okay. Thanks."

"I'm going out to the trailer. You want to go with me?"

Baa! Baa!

"You go ahead, Doc." She smiled. "It sounds like dinner time. I'll tend to the sheep and then see about throwing something together for everyone else."

Agent Brooke threw a fresh bale of hay over the rail and filled the water pan. She looked around the pen.

"Hey! Doc! Have you seen the lambs?"

Doctor Housel stuck his head out the back of the trailer. "They're out here keeping Khamiel and Dr. Rosenthal from getting lonely."

"Just checking, I'm going up now." She petted the ewe's head and went to the elevator.

Stan had changed into combat fatigues. She found him standing on the porch holding a laser sighted, modified MP-5A automatic weapon and around his waist, he carried an old WWII M-911 45 cal pistol.

"Are you trying to make yourself a target?" Agent Brooke stepped up beside him. "I hope you are at least wearing your vest."

"Better if I get it, than another member of my team."

"You keep talking like that, Freeman, and I'll be damned if I won't shoot you myself."

Stan grinned. “The paper work isn’t worth it.”

“I’m going to scrounge around in the kitchen. The medical team needs to eat.” She placed her hand on his arm. “You want me to fix you anything?”

“Go ahead, I’m fine.” He stepped off the porch and headed for the tree line. “I’ll do a perimeter check.”

She watched him get closer and closer to the woods. “Come on, Stan. Tell them you’re coming.”

He stepped into the woods.

“Damn you, Freeman.” She keyed her transmitter.

“Viper One to all posts.” Agent Brooke’s voice crackled with hostility. “Heads up! Viper is on the move—repeat Viper is on the move. Verify and confirm target before engaging.”

One by one, each member of the team acknowledged the call.

She went back into the house. “Damn fool, I know love is supposed to be blind, but did it have to turn him dumb too.”

Stan entered the tree line and keyed the mike. “This is Viper, just to make sure you’re awake out here, check your locators.” He reached down and turned his GPS transmitter off.

“Oh, shit!” Stan smirked as his earpiece crackled. “Heads up, he’s gone SEAL on us.”

Stan criss-crossed the security perimeter like a ghost. He found a giant oak and sat down with his back against the tree.

“Anyone see anything?”

“I ain’t seen shit out here since that damn turkey tried to peck my eye out.”

“If you hadn’t been flirting with the hen, that tom wouldn’t have gotten jealous.”

"Where the fuck is Viper?"

"He's probably back at the house sipping on a Long Island Iced Tea."

Stan chuckled at the banter in his earpiece. He pushed the switch for the GPS transmitter.

"Ahh! Shit! Viper's outside."

"Son-of-a-bitch!"

"At least I got the turkey. Does that count?"

Stan keyed his mike. "Okay boys and girls. If I can find the holes in the fence during the day, it's for damn sure someone can find them at night. Tighten it up."

"Viper One, patient status?"

"Temp down another half degree, BP 250 over 120. Brain activity is picking up rapidly. Patient is—unresponsive."

"Copy." Stan closed his eyes for a moment trying to clear his vision. "Viper out."

He lifted his hand into the air, closed his fingers into a fist and hit the ground beside him.

"You okay, Viper?" He recognized the voice of the other female on the team, the one who had raced through a firestorm of bullets and pulled him to safety.

"I'm good, Viper Five." He picked up a pine needle, stuck it his mouth and chewed on it.

Stan took a deep breath. He should have felt at home with the spicy fresh scent of the pine trees and the damp musty earth around him. There should've been peace sitting in the midst of natures' tranquility, but his heart and mind were seventy feet underground where Khamiel fought for her life.

He stood, walked a couple yards and came to a faint trail. There at his feet lay a partially dusted over heel print. Someone had taken the time to obliterate their footsteps, but was not good enough on the effort. The footprints led to a tall tree.

He walked the circumference of the tree. Approximately thirty feet up, he spotted a small black box secured to a branch. Stan pulled his pistol from his holster and mentally drew two slanted eyes on the side of the box.

"Viper—going hot!"

The heel plate of MK-911 slammed into his palm. The box exploded under the impact of lead traveling a thousand feet per second.

Birds scattered from their trees. Squirrels scampered for their dens. A doe went crashing through the underbrush. The woods went deathly quiet.

He smiled. *Damn that felt good.*

His earpiece crackled. "Status?"

"Viper One," he picked up a black piece of plastic, "just doing a little house cleaning. Soon as I pick up the trash, I'm coming in.

"Whoever got the turkey, flash your GPS. I'm hungry."

He marked the spot of the flashing light and started toward it.

Stan reached the man and started laughing. Viper Seven's face and arms were covered with band-aids, and his shirtsleeve had been reduced to tattered shreds.

"Hey, it was self-defense."

"What's so funny, Viper? We can hear you clear across the clearing."

"Viper Five, do you have any extra band-aids? Viper Seven appears to need a couple."

"I'll run them over."

"Viper Seven thanks you." Stan grabbed the feet of the headless turkey, slung it over his shoulder and left the woods.

He got halfway to the house when female laughter drifted across the clearing.

"Anyone got more band-aids? I ran out."

One by one, the team members broke open their medical packs.

He handed the turkey to Agent Brooke and winked. "We need to give this bird a proper send off, he put up one hell of a fight."

Stan keyed his mike. "Now that we've had our laugh, listen up. You felt the explosion earlier, thankfully no one here was killed but—Viper Two is down. The driver who delivered the trauma unit was none other than our old *friend* with a new face, Leian Wooso. Our orders are to take the bitch alive, if possible. Chinese Intelligence wants her almost as bad as we do."

Stan paused to let the information sink in. "Just remember—if she's breathing—she's deadly. Viper out."

"I'll be in the lab. If you need anything have Max let me know."

"What's going on, Stan?" Brooke grabbed his arm. "What aren't you telling me?"

"Wooso defected."

"*Defected?*" Chelae's eyes widened. "Where to?"

"North Korea." He stepped into the elevator.

Chapter Twelve

Stan entered the lab and crossed the tiled floor to where Dr. Housel sat at one of the workstations.

Dr. Housel's eyes shifted over at him and then right back to the screen. "I know you want answers. The good news is...she's still alive and her temperature seems to have stabilized at 102 degrees."

He leaned against the counter where he could see more of Dr. Housel's face. "What's the bad news?"

"Brainwave activity is registering higher than anyone has ever seen recorded." He tapped his fingers against the screen. "Take a look. I've brought up some PET reference images."

"Pet as in dog or cat?" *Why the hell should I be interested in what a damn animal's brain does or* doesn't *do?*

"No," Dr. Housel laughed, "PET is an acronym for an image of the brain called positron-emission tomography. PET pinpoints areas of brain activity during particular behaviors. The first two images were taken with the person lying down and no outside activities to influence the tests."

Stan moved around to where he could see the screen. "So these are like base images."

"You could call them base-line. This first one is from a normal woman of average intelligence." He picked up a pencil and pointed to two areas on the screen. "These are the cerebrum lobes. Notice the amount of color. The blue indicates areas of low activity, red indicates areas of high activity and then you have different levels in-between indicated by the varying shades."

Another image popped up on screen. "This scan is from a highly intelligent woman, which just happens to have been taken when Dr. Marie Roche attended the university."

The difference was immediately discernable, even to Stan's untrained eye. "Let me guess, this is a scan of Khamiel's mother."

"Right you are." Dr. Housel winked. "Even though she was considered a brilliant woman, notice when she was resting, she only used a small portion of her brain."

Dr. Housel brought up an image that caused Stan to lean closer.

"This one is also of her mother, taken as she is working on a complex bio-chemistry problem—and this is a live picture of Khamiel's brain activity.

The difference between the scans was staggering. Bright pulsating red filled both cerebral lobes of Khamiel's scan.

"We believe this unprecedented brain activity is what's causing her elevated temperature and blood pressure. I think she is somehow self-regulating her temperature with the increased blood flow to the brain and dissipating it throughout her body, but that's just my theory."

"Is she still—can you still..." Stan couldn't bring himself to finish the question.

"Yes." Dr. Housel put his hand on Stan's arm. "She is still visible..."

Stan exhaled a long sigh.

"...but we don't know for how long. There is nothing in Max's files to indicate transition development. There could be a trigger point in her brain that activates the formula all at once, or it could be gradual as more skin cells mutate. We just don't know. "

"Thank you, Dr. Housel. I'm going out to see her now, if that's okay."

"Go ahead. Dr Rosenthal would probably appreciate the company."

Stan started toward the door. He stopped beside Dr. King's chair. Her head leaned forward and he bent over to look at her. Dr. King's eyes were closed.

"Dr. King." He shook her.

Her eyes opened, her head popped back and she looked around the lab. "I'm sorry. I must have dozed off."

"You look exhausted. Why don't you go up and get some rest?"

"No." She stood and stretched. "I'll just freshen up a bit and then go relieve Dr. Hines."

Dr. King staggered over to the emergency shower. Her fingers fumbled with the buttons of her smock and she tossed it aside. She removed her bra, panties and turned the water on.

So much for wondering if she was a natural redhead.

Stan looked around the lab. The only other person who appeared to have noticed Dr. King's behavior was Dr. Lasovich, who sat watching her with wishful longing in her eyes.

"There's some clean smocks in the cabinet." Stan hurried from the lab.

Baa! Baa!

"What's the matter, Ten? Did your baby abandon you?" He reached over the rail, found the ewe and scratched her head.

Baa!

"I don't think there's room for you in the trailer too."

He continued on to the trailer.

Doctor Rosenthal gave him a tired straight-lipped smile, shrugged his shoulders and turned his eyes back on his patient. An IV bottle hung from an overhead hook with a fast drip flowing to a tube going to her arm.

"What's with the IV, Doc?"

"Brain food." He glanced up at the monitor. "When the brain is active, it consumes glucose. She's burning it as fast as we put it in."

Stan sat on a stool beside the bed and held her hand. "What are her chances, Doc?"

He looked at his watch. "It's been twelve hours. I'd say her chance of living is good, but all we can do is hope."

Stan massaged her hand.

Baa!

"Do you want me to take the lambs back to the pen?"

"No." Doc shook his head. "They're fine right there. I just wish they would eat. Neither one of them has touched a bottle since this started."

Stan picked up a bottle of milk and stuck the nipple in Red's mouth. The lamb took one swallow, spit the nipple out and laid its head on Khamiel's stomach.

Baa!

"I know you don't feel like eating, but you have to try."

"It's no use," Dr Rosenthal sighed. "I just hope they can hold out as long as this takes."

Stan picked up a damp cloth and bathed Khamiel's face, neck and arms.

"While you're here, I'm going to stretch my legs and get rid of the coffee Agent Brooke has been forcing down my throat." Doc stood and stretched. "If you need anything, just give a shout."

"Khamiel, I'm right beside you. You've got to hold on and fight this a little longer—just don't give up on me."

He felt a slight squeeze on his fingers.

"Doc!" His heart leapt into overdrive. "Doc! Come quick!"

Doctors Rosenthal, Xynath and Housel came running out to the trailer.

"She squeezed my hand." He tried to temper his excitement. "I was talking to her and she squeezed my hand."

Doctor Xynath put his hand on Stan's shoulder. "I'm sorry, Stan. It's an involuntary reflex of the muscles."

He started to argue with the Indian Doctor, but the sympathetic expressions of understanding on Rosenthal and Housel's faces stopped him.

His enthusiasm crashed. His shoulders sagged. "Are you sure?" He searched their faces but found no sign of hope.

"Sorry for the false alarm."

The emotional letdown ripped through his heart. Stan turned his head away from the doctors. He chewed on his upper lip and blinked rapidly.

Dr. Xynath patted his shoulder. "I know it's difficult, but you have to be strong for her. When she comes around, she's going to need all the support she can get."

Dr. Rosenthal reached over and petted Red Ribbon. "These little lambs have made their choice. They're in this for the duration. Question is...are you?"

Stan drew her hand closer, kissed her fingers and sprinkled her skin with tears. "I'm in..." he turned his face to the doctors, "...for as long as it takes."

Rosenthal gave him a strong wink. "I figured you were."

Xynath flashed a pearly white smile.

Housel turned away. "We need to get back to the monitors."

They left and he leaned close to her ear. "Khamiel, if you can hear me, squeeze my hand—twice."

He waited with bated breath for her to respond.

Stan felt a slight tightening of her fingers and then another, stronger than the first.

"Thank God." Tears ran freely down his cheeks.

Minutes seemed like hours as he bathed her forehead and held her hand. The turkey sandwich Agent Brooke made sat off to the side, partially eaten and forgotten

Doc Rosenthal changed her IV bag and sat on the other side of the narrow hospital bed. "Did you know her mother?"

"No, not personally. I never heard of her until I was briefed about the Chameleon project.

"Brilliant mind, but a loner. Not many people knew she had a daughter. I wonder why she never married."

"Hard to say." Stan laid Khamiel's hand on the bed. "I've got to up and...ah...check on my team. I won't be gone long."

"Take your time, we're not going anywhere."

Stan hurried to the elevator and shot toward the surface. He entered the kitchen, picked up the phone book and dialed.

"Hello, Doctor Davidson. This is Agent Freeman, I'm—"

"Son, do you realize what time it is. It's after midnight."

"Khamiel had an accident. I thought you might want to be here."

“Thank you.”

The line went dead.

He keyed his mike. “Viper, anyone awake out there?”

“Viper Three, Squad A on watch. Perimeter tight.”

“In about an hour there will be a car approaching. Single occupant, elderly, a Dr. Davidson. Make sure he’s alone and let him pass.”

“Viper Three copies.”

“Viper out.”

“Are you going to get some sleep?” Chelae sat on the floor with her back against the wall.

“I don’t know—maybe.”

She pulled her feet underneath her and stood. “Since I was so rudely awakened, I might as well make a perimeter check.

“Coffee was fresh an hour ago.” She picked up her night vision goggles and her rifle. “If you’re going back down, they might appreciate it.”

“Thanks, Chelae.” He picked up the pot. “Thanks for fixing the food, too.”

“Ah, hell,” she gave a half-effort of a wave and opened the door, “it was nothing. I didn’t have anything else to do except nursemaid a den of vipers.”

Chelae left the house and he carried the pot to the elevator.

Stan got to the lab and looked around in surprise. Everyone had crashed except for Sonya, who smiled at him from the emergency shower.

“Thanks, I could use some of that. My cup is over at the spectrum analyzer.” She rinsed the soap off, dried and slipped on a lab coat. “These coats are so neat the way they change color.”

Stan filled her cup and set the pot on a warmer. “Any change in her development?”

“Latest PET scan shows brain activity is about the same—maybe a little less.” She buttoned the coat as she approached her chair. “BP is dropping, but still elevated above normal.” Sonya picked up her cup and took a sip. “Ahh, thanks I needed that.”

She paused with her hand holding the cup in mid-air. “Where was I? Oh, yes. Her skin saturation is about seventy percent.”

He tilted his head to the side and looked at her intently. “Are you going to make it?”

“Sure, as long as I don’t sit down.” Her lips lifted in a lopsided, worn-out smile. “I’ll wake one of the others in a couple hours and then I’ll get some rest, which is what you should be doing.”

“I don’t think I could get much sleep right now.”

“There’s nothing we can do.” She lifted the cup to her lips. “Whatever happens will happen.”

“Yes, there is. When she wakes up, I can be there for her.”

“You will be, Stan.” Sonya laid her hand on his arm. “We’ll all be here.”

“Thanks. You don’t know how much I appreciate it. I think I’d go nuts here by myself. I’m going out to the trailer.” He started to walk away and stopped. “I almost forgot. There will be an older man coming down in about an hour. Would you show him to the trailer?”

“A friend of Khamiel’s?” She turned her attention back to the screens.

“If I’m not out in left field on this one, he’s her father.”

Sonya nearly dropped her cup. "I didn't think she knew her father."

Stan continued on toward the door. "She doesn't."

Doc Rosenthal lifted his head as Stan entered the Mobile Trauma Unit. There were bags under his eyes that Stan hadn't noticed before.

The man's gaze shifted to the monitors and slowly scanned the information. He reached over and held her wrist for a moment and then stood, arched his back and stretched.

Doc picked up his cup. "Long night."

Stan poured the steaming hot liquid into his cup and then into his own. "Doesn't look like it's going to get any shorter."

"I'm afraid you're right." Doc lifted his cup to his lips and inhaled the rich aroma. A smile of satisfaction lifted the corners of his lips. He took a sip and sighed. "There are still a lot of hours left before she's out of the woods. You might as well get some rest, if you can."

"I will. I'm waiting for someone to get here. A friend of her mother's."

Doc changed the IV bag and annotated a chart. "Suit yourself. I'm going to finish this cup and close my eyes for a few minutes. Maybe I can get the sand out."

He sat down and leaned his chair back against the trailer wall.

"Okay, Doc. I'll let you know if anything crazy starts happening on the monitors."

A few minutes later, Doc's eyes were closed and his chin rested on his chest.

Stan rescued the coffee cup and set it out of the way.

He held Khamiel's hand as he watched the IV bag; drip, drip, drip, drip. Stan leaned over and kissed her on the lips.

Beep! Beep! Beep! Beep!

The front legs of Doc's chair hit the floor with a crash. His eyes flew to the monitor and then to Khamiel. He reset the alarm.

"What did you do?" he demanded. "Her heart rate just spiked."

Sonya came running into the trailer.

"I didn't do anything. I just kissed her."

"Kiss her again!" Sonya said with excitement.

His lips touched hers.

Beep! Beep! Beep! Beep!

Doctor Rosenthal ran his fingers through his thinning hair. "I'll be damned."

"This is fantastic!" Sonya ran back toward the lab. "I'll tell the others."

Stan smiled at Rosenthal as they both wiped moisture from their eyes.

Within minutes, the rest of the medical team was crowded into the trailer. There wasn't a tired face or a dry eye among them.

Stan saw Doc Davidson come into the storage room.

"Over here." Stan waved.

He made the introductions and explained what happened. "I'm sorry about not calling you earlier. Things have been so hectic around here, I just didn't think of it sooner."

"No reason you should have, but I'm glad you called."

Sonya caught his attention, tilted her head at Khamiel and then at Doc Davidson. She moved closer to Stan. "You could be right," she whispered.

As Doc Davidson listened to the briefing of Khamiel's condition and development, he seemed to age before their eyes. Worry lines deepened in his brow. His eyes misted over and glistened in the bright light. He held his hands together in a white-knuckled, fingers interlaced attitude of prayer.

Stan put his hand on Doc's shoulder. "They want to run some more tests. Why don't we go up to the kitchen and I'll put on a pot of your special coffee."

Davidson sat in the chair for an eternity of seconds without acknowledging that he had heard a thing. He unfolded his hands, one finger at a time, reached over to the bed and brushed his fingers across Khamiel's cheek.

"Take your time," Stan spoke in a soft whisper. "I'll get the pot going." He left the trailer. *Maybe calling him wasn't such a good idea. Doc having a stroke or heart attack is the last thing we need right now.*

Stan entered the kitchen and turned on the light.

"What is this," Chelae grumbled as she shielded her eyes from the light and grabbed her things. "Grand fucking Central Station?"

"Where are you going?"

"Outside, where I'm going to shoot the asshole who wakes me up before the next perimeter check is due."

The door slammed behind her.

The elevator opened as the last of the water gurgled through the pot. Doc Davidson had a faraway look in his eyes. His posture slumped in deep sadness and regret as he rested his arms on the table.

Stan set a cup of Doc Davidson's chicory coffee on the table. "I'm sorry I had to be the bearer of bad news."

Doc glanced up at him and then his sorrowful gaze dropped back to the scarred wooden table.

"Must have been a heavy burden to carry all these years. Watching from the sidelines as she grew up...your wife couldn't have children, could she?"

Davidson shook his head.

"This was Marie's idea, wasn't it?" Stan continued, guessing...hoping he was somewhere near the truth. "She didn't want to ruin your marriage over a brief affair because she knew you loved your wife and, besides, she was already married—to her work."

A large crystal drop pooled in Davidson's eye and then fell to the table.

The tears in the old man's eyes told Stan that he was right. "It's eaten you up for years, almost to the point of resentment. Your wife was sick and slowly dying. You loved Marie, but she kept from you the one thing more important to you than life itself—*your* daughter—who doesn't even bear your name."

Doc cradled his head on his arm. His shoulders shook. "She didn't want Khamiel to know," he sobbed.

"Go ahead, Doc." He reached across the table and laid his hand on the old man's arm. "If anyone has a reason to grieve tonight, I guess it's you. God knows you've earned it. Just remember one thing...she's still alive. You're daughter is still alive and needs you now more than ever."

"It's too late now." Doc raised his tear-stained face. "It's too late."

"As long as she's breathing, Doc, it's *never* too late. You can wait and hope she wakes up, or you can tell her now. Ask her forgiveness. Let her know you're here for her."

Stan got up from the table and went to the elevator. “The choice is up to you.”

Chapter Thirteen

A void surrounded Khamiel, empty of sound, sight or the faintest glimmer of any light. Confusion wrapped her within its tangled web. She was running—yet standing still—fleeing from what or whom she couldn't tell. If only she had a reference point to guide her—but the void around her remained blacker than any night.

The voices came, faceless...nameless...dancing voices. She reached for them, but they were never there. She cried out to them, but they did not hear.

Surely, someone must care.

Suddenly, hands were prodding, poking—impersonal hands touching her in personal places. She didn't want their fingers on her. Whatever they were doing, she wanted them to stop. A hand touched her—different from the others. Strong, warm fingers bathed her face and gently soothed her fears.

This hand cared—it was her guiding light. Adrift in a sea of uncertain darkness, she was no longer alone.

Please! Don't go.

A voice filled with compassion reached inside and caressed her soul.

"Squeeze my hand, I won't let go."

Nearer and brighter, the light drew closer. Its warmth touched her. Darkness turned to a heavy curtain of gray.

A shadow of a man appeared. In the man's arms so loving and kind, he held a baby who laughed and giggled so free.

I know the man but how can this be—for I see now, the baby is me.

She looked into his eyes and the depths of his burdened soul.

He spoke to her. His voice etched with sorrow and regret. "Can you find it in your heart to forgive an old fool?"

Khamiel opened her eyes.

Tears coursed down the old man's cheeks.

She whispered, "Father, there is nothing to forgive."

"Khamiel!" Stan cried. "Thank God, you're awake."

Dr. Davidson's eyes widened in alarm and his hold on her hand tightened, as if he were trying to prove to himself that she was real or afraid she would try to run away.

Stan needed a shave. Fatigue and worry showed in the lines of his face.

"Why are you dressed like that?" She found she couldn't talk above a whisper.

"Do you remember the accident?"

"Yes, of course I do." She looked around at the strange faces. "Who are all these people? Where am I?"

"You are in your mother's underground lab, Khamiel. This is a Mobile Trauma Unit. These are Doctors Housel, Rosenthal, King, Lasovich and Hines.

The blonde, blue-eyed woman with a stethoscope around her neck stepped closer to the bed and smiled. "Please, call me

Sonya. Dear, you've been through a hell of an ordeal, and it's not over yet."

"How did all this get here in—" she looked up a clock on the wall, "—two hours?"

"Khamiel," Stan's voice broke with emotion, "your accident was yesterday morning."

"Yesterday!" She reached out her hand to him, but he made no move to take it or even notice it was there.

The formula. He can't see me. The realization sent a cold foreboding chill up her spine.

She felt something warm and soft next to her legs. Khamiel lifted her head. "I can see the lambs."

"They haven't left your side since we brought you down." His left arm extended and she latched onto his hand.

"You held my hand most of the night."

"Lie still, my dear," Sonya's soft voice warned. "You have IV's in both arms and I'm not sure I can start another, if you pull those out."

"You're wearing one of my mother's lab coats." Her fingers clutched the sleeve and she heard a collective gasp from the others in the compact trailer.

"Looks like I have the touch," she murmured.

She turned her head to look at tired face of the old man. "Before I woke up, I had a dream. You held me when I was a little baby. Is it true?"

His glistening eyes overflowed. "Yes, Khamiel. It's true. I'm your father."

"I was so afraid that I when I woke, it would all be gone." She pulled his hand to her lips and kissed his fingers. "I'm glad you're my father." Tears coursed down her temples and soaked into the sheet.

"Khamiel, how do you feel now?" Dr. Sonya wiped tears from her face.

"Thankful to be alive...and hungry!"

Several of the people around her laughed.

"That's a good sign." Sonya turned her head. "Stan, if you could see about getting something for her."

"I'm in the road here." Doc Davidson stood. "I'll go up with you, Stan."

"Dad—" The word sounded foreign coming from her lips. "Try to get some rest. We'll talk later."

"I'd like that." He gave her hand a squeeze. He left the trailer with Stan.

Dr. Housel turned his face from a computer screen. "Khamiel, we have been monitoring your condition since we arrived. I think we can unhook the IV's, but I want to leave one of the catheters in for now."

"Might as well, I suspect that I've been a lab-rat for the last twenty-four hours, so a few hours more won't matter."

Dr. Housel motioned for the others to leave. "Ms. Roche, we are going to do all we can to find an antidote for the Chameleon Formula. Right now, we don't even know if it can be reversed."

"Thank you for everything you're done. I wish I could be of more help but I know very little about my mother's work."

"Why don't you just lie here and rest? After you eat, if you feel up to it, we'll see about getting out of bed and moving around."

"I feel fine, now," she protested.

Sonya removed the IV lines. "You gave us a scare. There were times we weren't sure you were going to make it."

"I can assure you, I felt the same way."

"Do you feel any—different? Notice anything you can put your finger on?" she asked.

"Other than being able to see the lambs, I'm not sure. Maybe, I should ask you the same question."

Sonya's eyes shifted. "The only thing I can see for certain is your hair. That will take the longest to be altered by the formula."

"That makes sense. Only the new hair will be altered as it grows." She thought for a moment. "Unless I cut it all off."

"Cut it off!" Sonya's eyes opened wider. "Girl, why would you want to do that?"

"What's the use of being able to blend in with my surroundings, if you can see my hair?"

"Wow." She laughed. "You're taking this a lot more tranquil than I would."

Khamiel swung her legs over the edge of the bed and tried to sit up. "Will ranting obscenities, screaming or throwing a fit change what I am or have become?"

"No." Sonya helped her. "It won't."

"Then those would be wasted efforts, energy and time."

Sonya reached up and smoothed Khamiel's hair. "You have such beautiful hair."

"Cut it off," Khamiel ordered.

Sonya lowered her gaze. "All of it?"

"If you can see it—shave it. I don't want to walk around looking like the tail end of a rabbit going in reverse."

"Why not cover it instead?" Sonya asked. "Take a lab coat and make a hood. It wouldn't take long. I'd be glad to do it for you."

“I’m sure you have other things to do that are more important.” She eased her left foot to the floor and then her right.

“Careful, your whole body has been altered and we don’t know to what extent.” Sonya held her arms. “I love to sew. Please, let me do this for you.”

“Okay, if it will make you happy, go ahead.”

“Thank you, I think this will be a perfect solution.” Sonya leaned closer. “I just noticed something; I can see your pupils.”

“They weren’t affected by the formula?”

Sonya pulled a small flashlight from a drawer and moved it across Khamiel’s eyes. “Hmm, apparently not. Sit back down and let me make a couple quick checks.”

Khamiel sighed and sat down.

“Now, close your eyes. Wow! That’s amazing. You go back to your normal skin tone.”

“Khamiel!” Stan hurried into the trailer. “You’re visible.”

She laughed.” “Now you see me.” She opened her eyes and her skin tone blended into that of the things around her. “Now you don’t.”

Khamiel noticed she could see everyone with equal clarity without turning her head.

“She’s just full of surprises.” Sonya turned her head toward Stan. “She wanted me to shave all her hair off, but I convinced her to let me make a hood from one of the lab coats.”

“Well, if she changes her mind...” he wiggled his eyebrows and smiled, “...I’ll be glad to help.”

Sonya dropped her gaze to Khamiel’s bushy black pubic hair. “I’ll just bet you would.”

“That’s an offer I might not be able to refuse. Oh, wow, I smell—food?” Khamiel licked her lips.

Stan and Sonya laughed.

"What's so funny?"

"Stan, you tell her."

He handed her a plate of turkey. "When you licked your lips, it looked like a tongue came out of the wall and disappeared again."

"This is just great, not only do I have to keep my head and pussy covered, but I can't stick my tongue out at anyone."

Sonya shook her head. "Stan, if you'll stay here with Khamiel, I'll get her a lab coat."

"Go ahead. Max and I can keep an eye on her."

"Speaking of Max," Khamiel paused as she swallowed her food. "How did you get all these people past his security?"

He smiled. "Through a back door override command disk."

"I bet he didn't like that." She took another bite. "Where do we go from here?"

"I like that?" He grinned. "You said *'we'*."

"I was speaking of everyone in general. I don't think there can be a *'we'*, as in *us*." Her heart twisted in agony. "There might not have been anyway, but now—there's no way it would work."

Stan's grin disappeared. His jaw muscles tightened, pulling his lips into a tight thin line. The pupils of his eyes constricted to pinpoint black dots. The fingers that had been so tender in their loving caresses slowly closed into angry fists.

This was a side of Stan she hadn't seen. Had she pushed him too far? Was he capable of physically harming her after what they had shared?

"Doc, somebody, get in here—now!"

Stan's eyes opened wider.

She moved away from him.

"I'll help you lie down," Stan said as he took hold of her arm. "The doctors will be here in a minute."

"I don't want to lie down." She jerked free of his fingers. "Let go!"

Dr. King entered the trailer at a run. "Stan, stop! Back away from her."

"Khamiel, calm down. No one's going to hurt you. Take a couple deep breaths and you will be fine."

"How many times do I have to tell you? I feel fine," she lied. She felt closed in, trapped with the other doctors crowding into the cramped quarters of the trailer.

"Khamiel, look in the mirror," Stan pleaded. "Please."

Her left eye focused on the mirror. She gasped at her reflection. "Why is my skin—black?"

"It's the Chameleon formula," Tracy announced. "When a chameleon is angered or frightened, its skin turns dark brown or black."

"Khamiel." Sonya handed her a lab coat. "A couple minutes ago, everything was fine. What happened while I was gone?"

Khamiel looked at Stan. "Nothing." She put the coat on and buttoned it. The material turned black and then slowly blended with the interior of the trailer.

Sonya turned to Stan. "You were out here with her. What did you say or do?"

"That's a typical woman's response." He lifted his hands in the air. "She says '*nothing*', so automatically, it's my damn fault."

Stan turned and walked away. "I need some fresh air."

A tiny piece of Khamiel's heart broke.

"Wait, Stan!" Tracy stepped in front of him. "Like it or not, we're all in this together. Running away is only going to compound the problems. One thing we can all agree on...the Chameleon formula is altering more than just her skin."

"What's causing it?" Khamiel asked.

"Excuse me." Dr. Lewis Xynath cleared his throat. "It could be an intricate part of the DNA itself. Something that wasn't seen and thus not removed."

"Which means precisely what?" Stan leaned against the wall.

"She could have other Chameleon characteristics as well."

"Hey! Just because you can't see me..." she closed her eyes, "...doesn't mean I'm not here."

"Exactly my point." Lewis beamed. "You just shut down the Chameleon by closing your eyes. You made the conscious decision to be seen."

Stan scratched his head. "I'm not following you, Lewis."

"I think I am." Dr. Hines smiled. "We're forgetting the power of the human brain over the reptile."

"So, when Khamiel pushed me away, it was actually the Chameleon in her."

"A chameleon by nature is a loner, living alone in their tree except when coming together for the purpose of mating. So it is..." Lewis paused, "...definitely a strong possibility."

"Mood swings could be horrific," Sonya suggested.

"Even violent," Dr Housel added.

"At least until—" Khamiel folded her arms across her breasts— "I gain control of the Chameleon."

"Let's try an experiment." Sonya smiled with enthusiasm.

"What?" Stan and Khamiel both asked at the same time.

Sonya turned to Stan. "Kiss her."

"What!" Khamiel shrieked.

"A wonderful idea," Tracy agreed.

"Have her think warm sensuous thoughts first," Dr. Hines suggested. "It might help us determine to what depth her emotions are controlled by the Chameleon."

"Even better." Sonya had a devilish twinkle in her eye.

"Don't I have a say in this?" Khamiel objected.

"No!" All five members of the medical team spoke at once.

"I...I don't believe this," she stammered. "You're all just a bunch of...of voyeuristic perverts. For, God's sake, Stan, you can't honestly want to go along with this. Can you?"

She looked at him and knew the answer. Desire simmered within his eyes. The thought of kissing her like this, with an audience, excited him—turned him on.

Khamiel licked her dry lips as he pushed away from the wall.

Hell, yes I want this. I'll stoop to about anything to hold you again. Stan's breath caught as her skin and lab coat turned a soft pastel blue.

He moved closer, lifted his hand and let his fingers lightly glide over her warm flesh from her chin to her right ear.

The light blue tint of her skin darkened.

His fingers traced up and around the outer edge of her ear.

The rise and fall of her breasts beneath her lab coat quickened.

Stan's fingers gently clasped her neck and drew her closer. Their lips met, cautiously at first and then with more passion.

He broke the kiss and leaned back. Khamiel's body glowed with a deeper, brighter blue. Stan turned his head. The others had left the trailer, but he knew they were probably watching on the lab monitors. For her sake, he had to put the brakes on the passion.

Khamiel backed him against the bed. Her lips sought his as her fingers tore at his belt and loosened his pants. He opened his mouth to stop her but she took advantage and her tongue darted between his lips. His pants fell down around his ankles.

She began to whimper, moan and rub her body up and down against him.

Stan put his hands on her shoulders and pushed her away. "Khamiel, the cameras."

"Fuck the cameras." Her fingers flew down the buttons of her lab coat and she dropped it on the floor. "I want you right here— right now."

Khamiel tore the rest of his clothes off, pushed him backward onto the bed and straddled his hips. She took his cock inside her with one hard downward thrust of her hips.

She may have retained the shape, feel and even the passion of the sexy Khamiel, but the sensuously erotic, pulsating glow of her skin sent a dire warning to his blood starved brain.

This was *not* Khamiel.

She took hold of his hands and lifted them to her breasts.

Fine dark lines, almost purple, appeared in her skin and then began turning pink.

It might have been her body, but she was not in control.

Her nipples went from electric blue, to purple and finally to a bright fiery red.

In his mind, Stan rationalized that in all practicality, and every improbable sense of the word, his cock was buried inside a reptile—a chameleon.

His erection died, deflated like a popped balloon.

Chapter Fourteen

His hands grabbed her around her waist, picked her up and almost flung her from the small bed. Khamiel stumbled backwards, started to fall and twisted her body in mid-air. She landed in a crouch on her hands and toes.

The blue tint of her skin darkened. "What the hell did you do that for?"

Stan scrambled off the bed and started pulling on his clothes.

"Damn you." She stood. "I asked you a question."

He turned his back to her and zipped his pants.

"Am I so revolting that you can't you even look at me?"

He picked up his utility belt and put it around his waist.

"What's the matter, Stan? Did you suddenly realize you were fucking a lizard?"

He flinched and she knew her barb struck home.

"Where's the macho warrior who was going to stand by me and protect me with his life, or did that promise only apply when I was, genetically—human."

Stan left the trailer.

"I told you it wouldn't work between us!" she yelled.

His long strides carried him quickly across the room and out the door.

"Go ahead, run away," she whispered. "I would if I could."

Khamiel sat on the edge of the bed. She felt dejected and empty on the inside.

"I'm sorry." Sonya sat down beside her. "I guess, maybe it was a mistake pushing you two together so soon."

"Better to have happened now and get it over with."

Baa!

Khamiel bent over, picked up her lamb and held him close. "I'll feed this one and then go out. I need some fresh air."

"I cut up one of your lab coats to use as a scarf." Sonya handed the material to her. "It's nothing fancy but if you go outside, it will hide your hair."

"Thank you." Khamiel tied it over her head.

Her legs felt wobbly, but she managed to walk a fairly straight line to the elevator. "What's the big idea of not eating," she scolded. "I'm going to fix you a bottle. Would you like that?"

Baa!

She entered the kitchen and stopped. "Who are you?"

"Agent Chelae Brooke." She smiled, came around the table and held out her hand. "I'm glad you are well enough to be up and around...even if I can't see you."

Baa!

"I've got a warm bottle here. I figured sooner or later the lamb would get hungry enough to eat."

Khamiel took Chelae's hand. "Nice to meet you. Are there any others here I should know about?"

"I take it Stan didn't tell you."

"Tell me about what?" She took the bottle and gave it to the lamb.

"A security team has a perimeter set up around the house." Chelae pulled out a chair for her. "Stan is outside somewhere, if you're looking for him."

"Was all this really necessary?" Khamiel ignored the offered chair. and smiled as the lamb clamped its mouth around the nipple.

"Stan seemed to think it was, and I agree."

Khamiel crossed the room, opened the door and stepped outside into the early gray of dawn. "Agent Brooke." She stepped back into the doorway and asked, "Where's the barn?"

"The barn?" Chelae picked up a dishrag and wiped the clean table.

"Yes, the barn. You know, that big red building that used to be down the road."

"Oh, *that* barn. It's not there anymore."

"Well, duh! I can see that." Khamiel marched back into the house. "What the hell happened to it?"

"After Stan took the Mobile Trauma Unit down, he left the tractor in the barn and a few minutes later—it exploded."

"A semi-tractor parked in my barn exploded all by its little lonesome self," she scoffed.

"It had help, of course."

"Oh, of course." The lamb squirmed and Khamiel repositioned the bottle. "How silly of me to think other wise."

"I can't begin to know what you've gone through, but—"

"You're right," Khamiel interrupted her, "you can't, so don't even try."

Chelae placed both hands flat on the table. "Listen, bitch! Stan hasn't slept or hardly eaten since your accident. If it weren't for him, you and everyone in the lab would be dead."

Khamiel hung her head and took a deep breath. "I'm sorry, I didn't mean to appear ungrateful, but I didn't ask Stan to bring in the Calvary or the medical team."

"If he hadn't, you *would* be dead by now."

Khamiel felt a cold chill and she shivered.

"The driver of the semi managed to get past our security, onto one of our planes and then killed one of our team members as she escaped. If she could do that, she could easily get past you and Max's security."

"I can handle my own."

Chelae slammed the palm of her hand on the table. "No, you couldn't have."

The door opened and Stan walked in. "Did you escape, or did they let you out of your cage?" He took a cup and filled it with steaming coffee.

"How did you know I was here?" She moved farther from the table.

He plopped into a chair. "Chelae had a pissed off expression as I came through the door and for a change, I knew I hadn't caused it."

"She told me that you lost one of your men, I'm sorry."

"It's all part of the job description." He took a sip from the cup. "Besides, it wasn't your fault." Stan set the cup down and rubbed his eyes with his thumb and forefinger.

"You've had enough of this stuff." Chelae took the cup and dumped the rest of his coffee. "Get some rest, I'll wake you if anything comes up."

He pushed away from the table and stood. "Don't forget to call in the Situation Report."

"You're starting to sound like a nagging husband," Chelae scolded with a shake of her finger. "Go to bed before I start treating you like one and smack you up the side of the head with a frying pan."

Khamiel frowned as he left the room without saying another word to her. "Would you like a massage?" she called after him as he shuffled down the hall.

"No." He closed the bedroom door behind him.

"What's eating him?"

"I figured you'd know." Chelae went to the window and looked out.

"Why would I? Remember, I was out for twenty-four hours."

Chelae turned and faced in her direction. "When he came up for your food, he was as happy as a kid with a new Christmas toy. A few minutes later he came back up and nearly took my head off before he stormed out the door."

"I guess you'll have to ask Stan." She ran her fingers through the lamb's soft wool. "I'm going to take this little fella back to his pen."

Stan went into the bathroom and tried to wash the sand and grit from his bloodshot eyes. He wanted nothing more than to lie down and not wake up until some time in the future. Her bed drew him like a siren from the storm-tossed sea.

He dried his face, tossed the towel onto the sink and went back to the kitchen. Both women had left the room. Stan picked up his modified MP-5 rifle.

"Agent Freeman, you don't need to take your weapon to bed with you."

"Who said I was going to bed?"

"Agent Brooke told you to get some sleep."

"I know what she told me."

"Where are you going?"

"To get some sleep." Stan crossed the faded linoleum floor.

"The bedroom is in the other direction."

He stepped onto the porch. The early morning Georgia sun inflamed the Eastern sky with giant swaths of red behind scattered gray clouds. He jogged, with a slight limp, to the tree line across the road.

"You have room in there for another body?" he whispered.

Viper Five jumped. "Damn you, Viper. One of these days you're going to get your ass shot sneaking around a hot perimeter."

"Been there, done that, I think I'll pass." He crawled into Janice's camouflaged position and stretched out next to her.

"Viper One just made a check."

Stan shifted and removed an acorn-sized rock. "I know."

She scooted over and gave him another couple of inches.

He scanned the forest as the rising sun pierced the trees and cast dancing shadows across the carpet of pine needles. A squirrel ran down a nearby tree, paused and then scampered off, looking for breakfast. Turkeys called from the treetops and then with a loud flapping of wings dropped to the ground.

"You look exhausted. Get some sleep, I'll keep watch."

He rolled onto his side with his back to her and closed his eyes.

Khamiel walked across the debris-strewn grass. Her new eyesight was amazing. It didn't seem to matter at what distance she saw things, she was able to focus on them with surprising clarity. She stopped, reached down and picked up a tiny fragment of an electronics board.

Almost instantly, her mind identified it as not belonging to the truck, a procedure that could have taken days in the FBI laboratory. She crisscrossed the field and found several more pieces of the cell phone used to detonate the explosives hidden inside the large vehicle.

Suddenly, from the headset that Chelae had insisted she wear, static erupted in a loud painful roar.

The kitchen door burst open. Chelae ran out of the house, fired her automatic weapon into the air and dropped flat on the ground.

Khamiel pulled her weapon from under her lab coat and hid behind a piece of the destroyed truck. Invisible or not, she could still catch a stray round should the bullets start flying across the field. Her coat and skin turned black. She forced her mind to concentrate on her surroundings and she began to slowly blend back in.

The static stopped and a dozen voices sounded at once inside her head, but the one voice she found herself listening for...was alarmingly absent.

✧✧✧

Gunshots pulled Stan out of a foggy stupor. He turned and stared into the cold, lifeless blue eyes of Viper Five. His hand went to her blood soaked jacket and then to his empty knife sheath to confirm the horrid truth; it was his knife, buried to the hilt between her breasts.

Blind rage swept over him. He reached for his knife, but couldn't find the strength to pull it from her chest.

Janice had been there beside him in the hospital. Whenever he had opened his eyes, she had been there. She'd bathed him, fed him, slept in the chair beside his bed, and this was how he repaid her.

Stan closed her eyes and pulled her into his arms. "I'm sorry Janice," he cried. "I'm sorry."

He stood and carried her limp body toward the house. He stepped out of the trees and three team members came charging from the woods to fall in around him, one on each side and one behind him covering the tree line with their weapons.

Chelae stood with wide-eyed, open-mouth confusion. "What happened, Stan?"

He sadly shook his head, carried her into the house and laid her body on the kitchen table. "I don't know."

"What do you mean, you don't know? That's *your* knife!" Chelae stepped back, lifted her weapon and flipped the safety off.

Chapter Fifteen

Khamiel stood on the porch with her hand on the latch of the screen door.

"What's going on out here?" Doc Davidson asked as he shuffled into the kitchen.

Chelae's weapon never wavered from Stan's chest. "Go back to your room Doc this doesn't concern you."

"I've been a medical examiner long enough to recognize a dead body when I see one."

"Doc. I don't want to force you to leave, but I will if I have to."

Doc grumbled and went back down the hall.

"Hand over your sidearm, Agent Freeman," Chelae ordered.

"Put your weapon down, Chelae." Stan removed his pistol and laid it on the table. "Surely you don't think I killed Janice."

"You were out there with her—alone. Do you deny that's your knife?"

"Yes, it's mine, but I didn't kill her." Stan looked down at his bloody hands. "Damn it, Chelae, stop and think about this for just one second. Janice was like a sister to me. Why the hell would I want to kill her?"

Khamiel couldn't believe what was taking place before her very eyes. The implications couldn't be true.

"You've been wired pretty tight ever since Khamiel's accident. Did you snap under the pressure?"

"Christ!" Stan grabbed his head with both hands and then dropped them to his side. "Would you listen to yourself? Think about what you are saying?"

"I don't want to believe it, Stan," Chelae paused. "I don't know what happened out there, but I'm looking at the cold hard facts. Speaking of Khamiel, any idea where she is?"

"She should be in the lab." Stan paced across the floor and then whirled around. "Max, replay the perimeter tapes in reverse."

Khamiel wished that she could see the monitor. Invisible or not, there was no way she could get inside without being noticed.

"Damn it!"

She heard Stan's curse.

"Mighty convenient to lose audio and video at the time of the murder. Don't you agree, Stan?" Chelae kept her weapon trained on him as he resumed pacing.

"You can't believe that I had something to do with this?" Stan shook his head. "This is absurd."

"You knew both frequencies. You had the opportunity. I haven't figured out a motive yet, but I will. In the meantime, why don't you have a seat. I'd feel a lot better if you were immobile."

"You can't be serious!" Stan exploded. "I don't believe this."

"Believe it, Stan." Chelae motioned with the barrel of her weapon. "You're under arrest for murder."

Khamiel watched through the screen door as Stan sat and the men who had escorted Stan to the house secured his hands behind his back. *Am I the only person here who hasn't gone insane? I've got to do something.*

She stepped off the porch, picked up a rock and threw it against the house. The screen door burst open as the men ran to investigate the noise.

As the door swung shut, Khamiel squeezed through the opening. She crept along the edge of the counter. "Safety your weapon and drop it, Agent Brooke."

"You don't want to do this, Khamiel. You'll be an accomplice to murder."

"Damn!" Stan's eyes squeezed shut and he hung his head. "Do you know what you are doing?"

Chelae dropped her weapon and Khamiel kicked it across the floor. "I'm sure you're about to tell me."

Chelae pleaded with her. "Just because you've fucked Stan, don't throw your life away over him."

"Just because his knife is stuck in Janice's body, don't assume he killed her." Khamiel took a kitchen knife and cut the heavy plastic straps from around Stan's wrists.

Stan rubbed his wrists. "You go through with this and your career with the FBI is over."

"My career ended with the accident."

The door opened.

"Come in boys and don't do anything stupid." She lifted her revolver to Chelae's head. "Stan, take their weapons and secure them."

The men looked wide-eyed at the pistol as it apparently floated in the air by itself.

Stan stood, his boots rooted to the floor.

"Damn it, Stan!" Khamiel yelled. "I know you didn't kill her, but while we are standing here, the real killer is out there waiting to strike again."

Stan took their weapons, radios and secured the three members of his team.

"Chelae, if you would be so kind to remove your utility belt." Khamiel stood a safe distance behind her and waited.

As soon as Chelae's belt hit the floor, Khamiel shoved her toward an empty chair. "Have a seat.

"Stan, you might as well tie her up, too."

"You were outside." Chelae sat and put her arms behind the chair. "Maybe you killed Janice."

Stan put the heavy plastic strap around her wrists and pulled it snug. "That makes as much sense as accusing me."

"You have a choice, Chelae." Khamiel walked over, grabbed her hair and pulled her head back. "We go after the killer and you guard the laboratory, or follow us and leave it unprotected. Somehow, I don't think the *president* would be happy if you choose the latter."

Stan added extra ammunition to his backpack and slung it over his shoulders. "We need to get going."

"I'll just be a minute." Khamiel picked up Chelae's belt and went to her room. She slipped on a pair of denim shorts underneath her lab coat, fastened the utility belt around her waist and holstered Chelae's 40mm Glock pistol.

She walked back into the kitchen and slipped her feet into an old dingy pair of running shoes. "Let's go."

They reached the perimeter and Stan picked up Janice's automatic weapon. He held the weapon out to Khamiel. "You might need this."

"How long do you think we have before they get loose?" She took the weapon from Stan and circled the spot where Janice was killed.

"Long enough for us to clear the area, if we hurry.

"Come on." She moved deeper into the woods. "This way."

"How do you know?" He fell in behind her.

"Easy, I spotted a couple broken pine needles."

"Maybe easy for you." She stopped suddenly and he ran into her. "Give me some warning next time. The only things I can see are your shoes and your weapon."

"Sorry, I'm still trying to get used to this myself." She slowly circled a tree. "Here's a foot print. By the size, I'd say the killer is a woman. She probably waited here to see what would happen when you discovered Janice's death."

"I figured it was her." He knelt down and examined the ground.

"You *know* the killer?"

"Yeah." Stan ran his fingers through his hair. "I know her. She's Leian Wooso, alias Lee Woo your mother's assistant for three years, alias *Han-Shi*—Chinese for Black Death—and now recently gone over to the North Koreans. She has another alias, but it's not important. I can't figure out why she would kill Janice and not me."

"Maybe, she's playing a game. Letting you know she could have killed you. It could be as rewarding to her as actually doing it. She humiliates you, gets you to doubt your instincts and you start making mistakes."

"Getting arrested for killing one of my own team members would be the ultimate humiliation." He stood and scanned the woods. "Plus it would take the focus off of you, making it easier to get the formula."

"How's your hip doing?"

"I'll survive." He reached for her weapon, grabbed her wrist and pulled her close. "Thanks for sticking your neck out back there. You didn't need to do that."

"Yes, I did. You promised Doc—my father, you would protect me." His sudden nearness quickened her pulse and she licked her lips. "Damn difficult to do from a jail cell."

Stan lowered his head. "And, I wouldn't have been able to do this." He gave her a quick kiss.

"We're not going to catch the murderous bitch if we stand here all day." She moved away and began searching the ground for clues.

"Take the lead, I'll be right behind you."

Khamiel followed the path through the trees, not so much on the almost indiscernible evidence of the killer's passing, but from half-forgotten childhood memories.

A squirrel scampered up a tree and barked its displeasure at being disturbed.

She lifted her weapon as a signal to stop and crouched down.

Stan crept up beside her.

"There's an old shack up ahead." She hid her weapon inside her coat. "I'll check it out."

"No, it's too dangerous. I'll go." Stan ordered and waited for a reply. "Khamiel...Khamiel—Damn it."

She approached the building and circled around to the front. A single set of footprints led off toward the water's edge.

Time had not been kind to the old fishing cabin. The glass in the single window was long gone. The door hung ajar on one hinge.

She moved closer, looked in and with her finger on the trigger of her weapon, entered the cabin.

Trash and debris littered the small room. Rusty mattress springs lay on the hand-made wooden bed frame, its cover and ticking long ago torn apart by animals. A tree had grown through the floor and pushed its way through the roof.

She heard a noise behind her. Khamiel whirled around.

Stan's eyes bore into hers. A scowl turned his lips into a thin compressed white line.

"It's empty," she sighed. "We missed her."

"You could have gotten yourself killed." He threw her shoes on the ground. "You *ever* pull a stunt like that again, and I'll beat your ass 'til you can't sit down."

"Did it ever cross your mind that as good as you are, I do have an advantage here."

"That's besides the point," he fumed.

"No!" She bent down and grabbed her shoes. "That is the point, not only because I am the ultimate in camouflage, but I grew up here."

His eyes opened wide and his lips puckered. "You *knew* about this place?"

"I had no idea it was still here. It doesn't look like much now." She turned around and saw the place through the eyes of a lonely young girl. "Once upon a time, it was a mystical castle. That tall oak tree was the tower where the beautiful princess waited for her prince charming to cross the moat and rescue her."

"Now that we've taken this trip down memory lane, may I remind you, we're on a mission to catch a killer?"

"We have a problem. Unless you have an inflatable raft in your backpack, this mission is on hold."

"If I can get a boat—" Stan turned and gazed out across the water, "—which direction would you go?"

The inside of the old fisherman's shack flashed through her mind. Although she had taken but a quick glance inside, every little detail became surprisingly clear. "I'd go down river."

"Now all we have to do is find a boat." Stan adjusted his pack. "Let's go."

He turned and started off down river.

She sat on the ground and pulled her shoes on. "Hey, wait for me!"

Khamiel jumped to her feet and ran to catch up.

Stan's limp didn't seem to slow him down as he wove his way through the trees near the water's edge. "What do you think you are going to do, flag down some fisherman and hitch a ride to town?"

"Not exactly," he hissed. "Keep it down. Sound travels a long distance over water."

"He's going to take one look at you in jungle camo, armed to the teeth and all you'll see of him is his wake."

Stan chuckled. "Guess I'll just have to shoot him."

"You can't do that!" She latched hold of his arm and spun him around. "You'll go to jail."

"I'm joking—relax."

Stan raised his hand, brushed the side of her breast and found her chin. He tipped her head up. "You trusted me back at the house, don't let it waver now."

She stood on tiptoe and kissed his cheek. "I still trust you."

"Good." He gave her a quick kiss on the forehead. "Now, can we please find a boat?"

Khamiel stepped back. “Well we won’t find one dilly-dallying here all afternoon.”

Stan shook his head and started off through the trees. “Next time, remind me to leave you at home.”

She followed Stan for close to an hour and was beginning to think that they were never going to spot a boat close to the shore when suddenly, he ducked behind a tree. There ahead of them, no more than ten yards off shore, sat a boat with a single gray-haired fisherman.

Stan shed his pack and laid his automatic rifle against the tree. “Stay here.”

“You know,” she whispered, “you can be a real pain in the ass.”

“Good, I’d hate to think I was losing my touch.”

She watched him creep closer to the water and then vanish as if the ground swallowed him.

“Damn, he is good.”

Khamiel grew impatient waiting. She couldn’t get his comment about shooting a man just to get his boat out of her mind. Was he joking, or had his obsession over catching this rogue Chinese agent finally pushed him over the edge?

She moved closer to the water where she could see and hear what was happening.

The fisherman laid his pole down. He stood, unzipped his pants and peed over the side.

Stan’s head broke the surface of the water. His hands grabbed the top of the gunnels and he pulled down with all his weight and slid over the side. The boat lurched to the left. The fisherman lost his balance and fell overboard.

"You fucking, son-of-a-bitch," the man screamed as he spit water out of his mouth and grabbed for his hat. "I'm going to kick your sorry, good-for-nothing ass."

Stan pulled his pistol and pointed it at the fisherman.

Khamiel watched with a lump of fear in her throat. She wanted to scream, but couldn't.

"I don't think you fully appreciate the situation. I'm with the Department of Homeland Security and I'm commandeering your boat to get down river."

"Like hell you are."

"Mister..." Stan took careful aim, "...you move and you're dead."

He fired.

The loud explosion reverberated across the water and pounded her heart with the force of a jackhammer.

Khamiel expected to see the man floating face down in the water. That he would actually swim toward his boat surprised her.

The man reached for the side of the boat. He hung on and tossed a six-foot snake into the boat. "Nice shot, thanks. I guess I owe you one."

Overcome with relief that the man was alive, Khamiel sagged against a tree.

"You're one of *them*," she heard the man exclaim. "I could have lived to be a hundred without seeing another one of those Omega patches."

Stan eyed the man cautiously. "Where did you see one of these before and how the hell do you know about Omega Sentry?"

The man chuckled. "Give an old man a hand, son. I'll never forget the day your *Omega's* sunk half the Korean Navy."

Stan secured his pistol. He gave the man a hand and pulled him into the boat. "You were there?"

"Damn straight! I'm Lieutenant Ron Blake, Well Deck Officer for the USS *Belleau-wood,* at your service. Damn shame I can't tell anyone about it or that amazing woman with them."

Stan laughed. "I'll tell Aleecia you remember her and I'm afraid this will be another one of those times which will require your complete secrecy."

"Hell, I wasn't born yesterday."

"My gear is in the woods." Stan paused. "I'm not alone."

Blake pulled up the anchor and looked toward the shoreline. "I didn't figure you were."

Khamiel took several deep calming breaths. She concentrated on the trees and underbrush around her. Her hands slowly changed from black to blend with the gray moss-covered tree that she leaned against.

Stan stood on the bow of the boat as it pulled up to the shore. He turned to Blake. "I'll just be a minute."

She picked up Stan's backpack, stepped away from the tree and threw it with all the strength she possessed.

The flying pack caught Stan in the chest, toppling him over backwards. He landed with a splash in the shallow water and the thick, gooey-black mud.

Ron Blake started laughing.

Stan spit water, tried to stand and lost his footing. He fell back into the mud.

Ron laughed harder and pounded the steering console of his boat.

"What the hell was that for?" Stan sputtered and wiped his face with a muddy hand.

She joined Ron in laughter. “For shooting at this poor defenseless man and nearly giving me a heart attack.”

Ron looked up and down the shoreline trying to see her.

“I was shooting at a snake.” Stan waded through the mud and tossed his backpack into the boat.

“How was I supposed to know that?” She stepped into the bow.

The boat rocked and Ron sobered. He looked at her shoes. “Would someone, please explain what is going on?”

Stan wiped as much mud from his clothes as he could. “Ron Blake, meet…the Chameleon.”

“I don’t see anyone,” he exclaimed with nervous anxiety in his voice.

“Relax, Mr. Blake.” She closed her eyes. “I assure you, I’m quite real.”

“Sweet Mother of God!” He exclaimed.

She felt the boat move as Stan climbed in and said, “Ron, now you understand the need for secrecy.”

Khamiel opened her eyes. “Sorry to startle you like this, Mr. Blake. Please don’t ask me to explain.”

Stan sat behind the boat’s console and started the engine.

“That’s—all right,” Ron stammered. “I’m not sure I want to know.”

Stan increased power to the engine and backed away from the shore.

“Stan, you don’t know the lake. Why don’t you let Mr. Blake drive? We might get there faster.”

“Where do you want to go?” Ron cautiously moved forward.

Khamiel smiled at the scared rabbit look on his face. His eyes glued on the only thing he could see…her shoes.

Stan got up and sat beside her.

Ron slipped into the seat.

She laid her automatic weapon in her lap. “Are you familiar with the Bridge View Motel?”

Ron’s eyes flickered nervously to the weapon. “Yes.”

“That’s where we’re headed.”

“How can you be sure?” Stan asked.

Ron added power to the engine and the boat moved off across the water.

“There was a matchbook from the hotel in the cabin.” She grabbed the material covering her hair to keep it from blowing off. “I figure that’s as good a place to start as any.”

“And, if they aren’t there?”

“Then we’re right back where we started.” She lifted her other hand and wiped a finger across his mud-smeared face, “Look at the bright side, at least we’ll have a roof over our heads and you will have a chance to clean up, although that may require some help to accomplish.”

Ron increased power and rather than shout over the noise, they lapsed into an uneasy silence.

The sun hung low in the sky and cast long shadows across the surface of *Lake Lanier* as they pulled up to the dock of the Bridge View Motel.

“You better let me check things out.” Khamiel slipped off her shoes. “You might attract some unwanted attention.”

“If they’re there, don’t do anything stupid,” Stan warned. “Come back and get me.”

“I will.” She leaned over and kissed a clean spot on his forehead.

Khamiel stepped onto the dock and started across the parking lot. A car came around the corner and headed straight for her. The car was scant feet from her when she realized the driver couldn't see her and she jumped out of the way.

She reached the motel office and looked inside. The room was empty and she opened the door. A bell sounded.

Khamiel hurried through the door and a man of Indian descent came out of a back room. He looked around, shrugged and left.

She stepped behind the counter and searched through the hotel records. A registration card with a bold signature caught her attention. The name, Joe Pecker, didn't mean anything to her, but the handwriting was unmistakable.

Khamiel hurried out of the office and back to the boat.

"I found them!" She jumped into the boat and picked up her automatic weapon. "They're registered in room fifteen."

Stan pulled a large bill from his wallet and handed it to Ron. "Thanks for the lift, Mr. Blake. This should cover the gas."

Ron took the bill and gave Stan a hurried salute. As soon as Stan hopped out, he jammed the throttle full open, spun the boat around and with a rooster tail of water ten feet high, sped through the 'No Wake Zone'.

"I forgot my shoes," Khamiel laughed in a soft whisper.

"We'll worry about shoes later." Stan shouldered his backpack. "Let's go."

They reached room fifteen and Stan pulled out two small thin strips of metal. Within seconds, he had the lock picked.

He slowly turned the handle and eased the door open.

Khamiel saw the clear plastic line at the top of the door. She shoved Stan out of the doorway. "No!"

A gunshot sounded from inside the room. The acid smell of cordite drifted through the partially opened door.

Chapter Sixteen

Stan burst through the door and took the room in at a glance. A Smith & Wesson 38 caliber revolver had been duct taped to the bed's headboard and a clear, monofilament line ran from the trigger back to the door.

Leon Haufmyer, securely tied to a chair and gagged, sat in the middle of the small hotel room with a large crimson stain spreading across his chest. His eyes held a scared, defeated, glassy, hollow gaze.

Knowing there wasn't much time, Stan went to his side and removed Leon's gag.

Leon coughed and blood dribbled from the corner of his mouth.

"Chair rigged," he warned. "Don't move me."

Stan looked under the seat and found a small package taped to the bottom.

"Tell Khamiel..." He coughed again. More blood flowed down his chin and dripped on his shirt. "...I'm sorry. No one was supposed to get hurt."

"Why, Leon?" Khamiel begged.

"Khamiel! Where are you?" Leon gasped. The harsh gurgle from his lungs sounded loud in the quiet room.

"I can't see you."

"I'm here, Leon."

She closed her eyes.

Leon's gaze focused on her and then the light in his eyes faded. His head fell forward and with a long eerie sigh, Leon Haufmyer died.

Stan reached over and closed Leon's lifeless eyes.

"He's gone."

She opened her eyes and Stan saw her tears as she faded from view.

Police sirens shattered the late afternoon quiet as several cars slid to a stop in the parking lot. Stan holstered his weapon and pulled his Homeland Security Shield from his pocket. "You better find someplace to lay low until this is over."

"I noticed room seven was empty. I'll help myself to the room key. I doubt anyone will be renting another room today."

"You there, in room fifteen! Come out with your hands up!"

"Good luck," Khamiel whispered and gave his arm a squeeze.

Stan lifted his hands and with his shield visible, stepped through the door.

"Don't shoot! I'm Agent Freeman, Homeland Security. There's an agent down inside. The chair is wired with explosives, probably *Semtex*."

Police officers, who had been approaching quickly, turned and ran back to their cars.

"Agent Freeman, please walk away from the building."

He followed the officer's instruction, thankful to be putting some distance between himself and the deadly package underneath Leon's chair.

Police officers scurried like frightened ants to empty the motel and move people to safety.

Khamiel edged down the side of the building as she tried to avoid contact with anyone. A man went running by, tripped over her foot and went sprawling onto the concrete. He scrambled to his feet, briefly looked behind him and then took off again.

She reached the office just as the door burst open. The manager along with his wife who held a naked, screaming, wet child ran from the building. Khamiel entered and quickly found the key to room seven. No one seemed to notice the door opening as she left.

This can't be happening! She watched in horror as Stan was handcuffed and shoved roughly into the back of a police car.

He looked through the side window. His eyes roamed the area and then stopped on the spot where she stood, as if he knew for certain where she was standing.

She saw him sigh and shrug his shoulders. His lips moved, "Sorry—she's won."

Her fingers tightened into closed fists. "I'll be damned if she has," Khamiel whispered.

Two policemen got in the front seat and the car pulled out of the parking lot.

She couldn't bear to see his down-turned lips and his long face of despair. Khamiel closed her eyes.

"Ms, you shouldn't be here. This area is off limits. There is a bomb in the building."

Damn! Think of something...quick! She groped around and found the man's arm. "Are you a police officer? In all the confusion, my dog ran off. Have you seen her?"

"No, I'm sorry. I didn't realize you were blind. Please, forgive me. I'll lead you to safety and then see if I can find your dog for you."

"Thank you, Officer. You are so kind. I hate to put you to any trouble, but I'd be lost without him."

"Ms, what kind of dog is it and what's his name?"

"Shit," she mumbled.

He laughed. "You named your dog Shit?"

"Ahh—no! I said Sheik...his name is Sheik and he's a blonde Labrador."

"Okay, Miz. Just put your hand on my arm and I'll get you clear of the hotel."

She breathed a huge sigh of relief as she allowed the officer to lead her away from the hotel. "I'm afraid all the excitement has made me tired. If you could find some place for me to sit where I won't be in the road, I'd deeply appreciate it."

"There is a bench here on the dock."

"That would be nice. Thank you so very much." She reached out, found the back of the bench and sat. "Don't worry about me, I'll be fine."

"If I see your dog, I'll bring her to you."

Now all she had to do was figure out how to get Stan out of jail.

In all the noise and confusion, she couldn't hear if anyone was close to her or not. Khamiel fussed and fumed at not knowing what went on around her. Should she dare open her eyes?

"Hey, Babe! What's a fine looking thing like you sitting out here all by yourself?"

Khamiel stiffened as the cocky voice intruded upon her mind. "I'm waiting for someone."

The man laughed. "I think you've been stood up. I'll just sit down here and keep you company."

"Please, don't bother," she bristled. "I want to be alone."

He sat beside her. His leg brushed against hers. "We are alone," he whispered. One of his hands touched her inner thigh, the other, the back of her neck.

Khamiel lifted her arm, opened her eyes and gave him an explosive, backward jab in the throat with her elbow. She reached across with her other arm, grabbed a handful of hair and jerked him off the bench. He did a somersault and landed on his back gasping for air.

He tried to sit up when the heel of her hand met his forehead. His head bounced off the boards once, and then his eyes crossed as he lay unmoving at her feet.

"You bastard." She spit the word out of her mouth. "I ought to castrate you, but Georgia has a law against cruelty to dumb animals."

She knelt beside him, patted down his pockets and removed his keys. "Thanks for the use of your vehicle."

Nobody had noticed her disappearance. Khamiel left the dock in search of her would-be assailant's vehicle. She pushed the locking button on the keyless entry fob and a pair of headlights flashed.

She approached the older SUV with caution. Its windows were heavily tinted making her ability to see inside difficult. Upon making sure her assailant didn't have an accomplice waiting inside, Khamiel opened the door and sat behind the steering wheel.

"The Chameleon to the rescue..." she whispered as she started the engine, "again."

A police car left the parking lot and she pulled out behind it. She hoped, with a little luck, she could follow it right to the station. Khamiel turned the dash lights off and let a couple cars get between them.

A traffic light changed and she jammed on the brake. She pounded the steering wheel and watched helplessly as the police car continued down the street.

"Come on, change. Damn slow-assed light," she fumed as she revved the engine.

A pedestrian stopped in the crosswalk and stared. He scratched his head, looked around and then stepped closer.

"Go away," she mumbled.

He was almost to the window.

The light turned green.

Khamiel leaned over and closed her eyes.

The man tapped on the driver's door window. "Sorry, I didn't see you in there."

She sat up in the seat, gave the man a frosty smile and stepped blindly on the gas. The SUV jumped forward into what she hoped was a clear path. She felt the front tire roll over something.

"You stupid bitch!" the man yelled.

Khamiel opened her eyes and smiled. The man shook his fist at her while jumping up and down on one foot in the middle of the street. She scanned the street ahead of her, but couldn't see the police car.

She pulled into a parking lot, got out and walked over to a pay phone. “Never a phone book around when you need one,” she grumbled and dialed information.

A few minutes later, she dialed the Gainesville Detention Center.

“Hello, this is Agent Roche with the FBI. An Agent Freeman was taken in for questioning concerning the Haufmyer murder this evening at the Bridge View Motel. Are you holding him at your facility?”

“One moment, Ms. Roche, I’ll check where he was taken.”

Khamiel knew the procedure. They were stalling to allow a phone trace and get an officer en route to her location.

Several long agonizing minutes later the person got back to her. “Agent, Freeman was taken to the police station at the Lake Shore Plaza.”

“Thank you.”

A police car sped around the corner, its tires howling in protest as it entered the parking lot. Two more slid to a stop and blocked the entrance. She left the receiver dangling and walked back to her borrowed SUV.

The first cruiser came to an abrupt stop. The officers bailed out with their weapons drawn and approached the phone booth.

Khamiel smiled.

“She has to be here. the sarge was talking to her as we pulled in.”

“Shit!” The second officer looked around frantically. “Where the hell did she go?”

“She couldn’t have gotten far. Call for additional backup. I’ll start checking vehicles.”

“Be careful.” The officer hung up the phone. “She’s armed.”

"You mean they're giving the FBI real weapons. What's this world coming to?"

"Ain't that the fucking truth? The guy they're holding downtown supposedly killed another agent and this one helped him get away. It's getting so you can't tell the good guys from bad."

One officer approached the vehicle, shined his flashlight around the interior and put his hand on the hood. "Hey, Joe! This engine is still hot."

"Run the plates."

Khamiel listened as he called in the license plate.

His eyes got big and he shifted his weight from one leg to another. "Joe! We got a hot one. The owner just reported it stolen from the Bridge View Motel."

"We know she's still here somewhere." Joe turned around in a slow circle. His flashlight probed the dark shadows. The other officer opened the passenger door of the van and cautiously looked in.

A car pulled up and stopped on the street. The driver got out and approached. "My cell phone is dead. Is it okay if I use the pay phone real quick?"

"This parking lot is secured." He stepped away from van leaving the door open. "There's another phone down the street two blocks."

Khamiel hurried out the open door. She couldn't believe her good luck as she ran over to the running vehicle.

"Thanks for the information, Officer." The man returned to his car, opened the door and paused. "Have a good night."

Khamiel dove through the open door and into the passenger seat.

The driver got in, closed the door and continued down the street.

She laid her hand on his arm. “Thanks for the lift, Mr. Blake.”

“Good thing I was in the area.” He chuckled. “They might have accidentally stumbled over you.”

“You just didn’t happen to be here, did you?”

“No.” He paused. “Where are we going?”

“The Lake Shore Plaza.”

He smiled. “I got back to the motel in time to see your little stunt on the pier.”

“Do you make it a habit of following strange women around town?”

“Sure, all the time.” He lifted his hand and placed his index finger to his lips. “But nobody else can see them.”

Khamiel laughed for the first time in hours. “I won’t tell a soul. Your secret is safe with me.”

“Where’s your special forces friend?” Ron asked.

“Damn fool went and got himself arrested.”

“And you’re going to...?”

“Get him out.” She finished his sentence for him.

Ron grinned and then broke out in laughter.

“What’s so funny?”

“This should to be interesting, to say the least.”

“Are you sorry you came back to the motel?”

Ron turned his head and winked. “Wouldn’t have missed this for all the fish in the lake.”

✧✧✧

Inside the tiny olive green interrogation room of the Lake Plaza Police Station, Stan Freeman sat at the single table and faced the large mirror, which he knew was actually a one-way glass window. Across the table from him sat an overweight detective with the glare in his eyes and the scowl of a pissed-off bulldog.

They had been sitting like this, eyeball-to-eyeball, for several long minutes. The fingers of the man's right hand closed into a tight fist. His nostrils flared with each breath.

Stan saw his rage reach the boiling point and steeled himself not to react.

The cop's fist slammed onto the table. "I don't know who the hell you are—and I don't rightly give a fuck."

He stood up with such abruptness his chair toppled over backward.

"What I don't like is some bureaucratic asshole in Washington telling *me* how to do my job."

The detective pounded the table again. "If you don't wipe that silly shit-eating grin off your face…I may forget my orders, and wipe it off for you."

Stan didn't rise to the detectives baiting but kept his voice level, controlled. "You could try, but I wouldn't recommend it."

"Oh, so you're a tough guy. Well, Mr. Tough Guy, before you leave here, I will have some answers. This is my house—you came into my house," he yelled as he pounded on the table, "and shit all over my floor. I have a dead federal agent on my hands, another one who may or may not be mentally stable out on my streets with a loaded weapon, and I don't even know which department you belong to."

The door opened and the police chief walked in. He held a coffee cup in each hand.

“Detective Gibbs, why don’t you leave us alone for awhile?”

Gibes snarled at the chief and Stan thought he was going to refuse, when he stormed out of the room and slammed the door.

“Agent Freeman.” The chief sat the cups on the table. “I want to apologize for my detective’s attitude. We don’t treat fellow law enforcement personnel that way.”

Stan took a sip and sat the cup back on the table. “Apology accepted.”

“If you take sugar or cream, I’ll have some brought in.”

Stan shook his head. “No thanks.”

“Is there anything you need, Agent Freeman?”

“Other than to let me go so I can find the killer—no.”

The chief leaned forward in his chair. “So, you know who it is?”

Stan took another sip of coffee as he thought about how much information he could safely feed the Gainesville Chief of Police. “Yeah, I know and, trust me on this one, Chief, you don’t want to get involved.”

“I’m already involved. Give me a name and description. I’ll get an All Points Bulletin out.”

Stan slowly turned the coffee cup around in circles. “Sorry, Chief. Afraid my superior would object.”

“Just who the hell are you with?”

It was Stan’s turn to lean over the table. He shifted his gaze around the small room and whispered. “If I told you, the agents coming for me would have to kill you.”

The chief laughed. "You *spooks* never change. You're always so damn melodramatic about your assignments.

"I hope you can understand my dilemma," the chief continued in a more serious tone. "I'm the one the Mayor comes to when law and order goes to hell in a hand basket. Personally, I don't like our mayor up my ass. I'd appreciate any information on this situation that you can give me."

"The killer is a woman," Stan whispered. "If I gave you her name and description, your officers have to be prepared to shoot her whenever and wherever they see her, without warning...*Bang!*"

His last word exploded inside the quiet room. The force of it set the chief back against his chair.

The chief blinked once, twice. His jaw dropped. "Where do you think you are, Agent Freeman? This isn't some third-world dictatorship. We have rules and regulations regarding the use of lethal force."

"Chief, by the time your men start to recognize her, she will have decided which weapon she will use. How she will use it is second nature to her. Before that recognition is complete..." Janice's lifeless face floated before Stan's eyes. His voice choked with suppressed emotion. "...your officers will be dead. That's why I'm not telling you, or your pet bulldog, a fucking thing."

A muscle twitched just under the chief's left eye. His tight-lipped frown and slightly narrowed eyes barely concealed his anger. He lifted his cup with white knuckled fingers and took a sip. The cup shook slightly as he set it back on the table.

Stan smiled.

The chief looked through him. "Detective Gibbs, come in here."

The door opened.

"Transfer the prisoner to another facility."

"Which one, Chief?"

"I don't care where he spends the night."

Gibbs's mouth twisted into a sinister smile. "Sure thing, Chief."

Alarm bells began to sound.

Someone in the building yelled, "Fire!"

The chief jumped up and ran to the door. Smoke billowed down the hall.

"Secure the prisoner!" he yelled as he ran from the room.

Gibbs pulled his handcuffs out of their leather belt pouch. "You heard the man."

Stan held his arms out in front of him.

"Damn, I hoped you were going to resist."

As Gibbs lifted his handcuffs to slap them around Stan's wrist, his knees buckled, his eyes rolled to the top of his head and he fell across the table.

Stan sprang from the chair. "Took you long enough to get here."

"Save the small talk for later." Khamiel grabbed his hand and pulled him toward the door. "There's a car waiting."

Hand in hand, amidst the smoke and confusion, they walked through the police station and out the front door. She tugged on his arm. "This way."

As they turned the corner, Stan looked over his shoulder. A black Hummer pulled up to the front of the building.

"I'm glad you showed up when you did. The posse just rode into town."

A car door opened and Khamiel shoved him inside. "Move over, we haven't got a moment to lose."

She piled in and landed on his lap.

"Drive!" she barked.

The car pulled away from the curb with a screech of tires.

Stan turned to the driver. "I won't ask how you came to be here, but I'm damn glad to see you." Stan wrapped an arm around Khamiel's waist.

Ron grinned. "Where to?"

"I don't have a clue. We lost our only lead. We need someplace to hole up for a day or two until I can sort this mess out."

Ron waited for a traffic light to change. "I know just the place."

Chapter Seventeen

Ron's split-level home sat on a bluff. Every room in the house had a commanding view of Lake Lanier. A lighted stairway clung to the side of the bluff leading to a private beach where a pier jutted into the black expanse of water. A powerful cabin cruiser and the smaller outboard they had used earlier gently rocked at their moorings.

"Looks like you've done all right for yourself." Stan leaned against the patio railing sipping a double whiskey on the rocks. "Navy retirement must be paying pretty good these days."

"Not that good." Ron chuckled. "My wife had a head on her shoulders for playing the stocks. Back in '05 when that home decorating queen went under, the wife was so damn sure she would rebound she bought all the stock she could get her hands on. Then she did it again in '07 when North Korea and Iran's saber rattling put the price of gold through the roof." As they went back inside, Ron commented. "I should sell the place, but what the hell, I like it and I can afford to keep it."

Stan sat on the couch and sighed. "This sure is a lot more comfortable than the accommodations at the police station."

Ron grinned as he freshened Stan's drink. "Bet they don't serve twenty-one-year-old sipping whiskey either."

“Here’s to true southern hospitality.” Stan lifted his glass. “It was beginning to look like I was going to be their guest, until you showed up with Khamiel.”

“It was nothing. She did all the work.”

Two towels floated into the room. Khamiel had one wrapped loosely around her waist, the other in a tight twist around her hair.

Ron did a double take, lifted his eyebrows and shook his head. “Think you’ll ever get used to this?”

“I don’t know, Ron.” After his last disastrous relationship, Stan had sworn off getting involved. He hadn’t known Khamiel very long but she had, with her caring and faith in him, put a crack in the wall he had built around his heart. In a startling revelation, he found himself wanting more than a short-term affair. “Maybe in ten to twenty years.”

He grinned and took another sip of his drink, enjoying the heady aroma and bite as it trickled slowly down his throat. “One thing’s for sure. Life would never be dull.”

Stan sat his drink on the ornate glass coffee table. The towel Khamiel had worn over her wet hair flew through the air and smacked him in the face.

Ron laughed. “I think, before the other towel gets thrown, I’ll turn in.” He drained his glass and set it on the table. “It’s been a long day and I’m not used to all this excitement.”

“Good night, Ron. Thanks again for everything.” Ron’s glass floated through the air toward the sink.

“You don’t need to do that.”

“It’s the least I can do for letting us spend a couple of days here.”

“You’re welcome to stay as long as you need to. With the wife gone and me working in Norfolk, the house is empty most of the time. Hell, I spend more time at sea now as a consultant for the shipyard than when I was on active duty." Ron winked. "Same job, just better pay."

With a surprising amount of pep in his step for being so tired, Ron headed off to bed. "I'll see you in the morning."

Khamiel dropped her other towel and sat on Stan's lap. "I was worried about you." She kissed his neck. "I'm not sure what I would've done if Ron hadn't given me a lift."

Soft warm kisses moved sensuously up his neck to his ear as her fingers unhooked the buttons of his shirt. Her skin began to change from its camouflage blend to a soft aqua-blue.

"I was scared that I might no be able to get you out," she murmured.

"You—scared?" He touched her knee and caressed her skin. His fingers moved in slow lazy circles up her leg. "I think you are an amazingly brave woman."

Her skin tone darkened.

She kissed his cheek. "I was so upset that it was all I could do to stay invisible."

"When the fire alarm sounded," Stan chuckled, "I don't think they would've noticed you if you had been yellow with black polka dots."

Khamiel kissed the side of his mouth. "Setting the trashcan on fire was an act of sheer desperation."

As he turned his head, their lips met in a soft, almost first kiss, of reverence. "Shear genius," he whispered.

Khamiel wrapped her arms around his neck. Her hard nipples pressed against his chest. "If it hadn't worked—"

Stan silenced her with a longer, deeper kiss. "But it did. It worked beautifully."

Eyes gleaming with warm sensual desire, she leaned back.

As if pulled by an irresistible force, his fingers gently closed around her breast.

Her beautiful little nose flared and her chest swelled.

Stan grinned, lowered his head and took one of her nipples, now the grayish-blue of a turbulent storm darkened sky, between his lips.

Khamiel's fingers grasped his hair. "*Ahh!*"

The heat of her desire filled his mouth. Orange-red pulsating flashes darted from her breast across her darkening flesh.

The harder he suckled on her breast, the redder the darts became.

Stan released her nipple. It glowed like a smoldering ember against her cobalt-blue skin.

With a grunt, he stood. Need and want overshadowed and drove away the pain in his hip. "I think we need to finish this in the bedroom."

"We're not there yet?" She snuggled closer and nibbled on his ear. "I need you."

The way she said, "you," in that low, sensuous whisper cut to the very fiber of his soul. His cock, already straining the seams of his camouflage pants, throbbed painfully for freedom.

He carried her into the bedroom.

Khamiel ran her fingers through his hair. "I hope this isn't going to be a repeat of last time."

Stan sat her in the middle of the bed. "No, it won't be."

She helped him out of his military style shirt.

"I've been meaning to ask you about that."

"Why?" He sat on the bed beside her and lifted his hand to her hair.

"I think a woman has the right to know why she gets thrown from the saddle in the middle of a ride."

His fingers glided sensuously down her neck, and with a feather-soft touch, circled her breasts. "I'd rather not talk about it."

"I saw myself in the mirror. It must have been one hell of a shock." Her hand cupped his erection and gave a playful squeeze.

Stan closed his eyes.

"Was that the reason?" she asked in a soft purr.

"No."

Through the material of his pants, she squeezed him again. "Are you sure?"

"No."

"Which is it?" Khamiel laughed. She pushed him back onto the bed with her finger. "No, that wasn't the reason, or no you aren't sure?"

"I don't know."

She undid his pants and lowered the zipper. His cock sprang from his shorts like a young Marine's salute upon seeing his first real officer.

Khamiel touched the tip of his cock with her finger and slowly ran her fingernail down to his balls.

Stan's hard muscular body shuddered.

She smiled. "What do you know?"

"I need you," he panted.

"I..." she lifted her finger in a slow circular motion up the length of his cock, "...didn't hear you."

"I need you," he gasped. "I want to be inside you."

She lowered her head and kissed the smooth tip of his cock. "Anything else?"

"Christ, woman!" Stan clutched the sheets as she took him in her mouth. "I want to see you light up like a neon sign and—and know I caused it."

She paused from caressing his rock-hard shaft long enough to ask, "Is that the only reason?"

"Do I need—another reason to make love to you?"

"No." Her tongue toyed and teased the head of his cock. "But it would be nice."

Khamiel parted her lips and grazed his flesh with her teeth.

Stan's hips levitated off the bed and she quickly jerked his pants down around his knees.

"Combat boots..." She deftly untied his boot laces. "You sure know how to impress a woman."

"Any woman," he asked in a quiet husky whisper, "or you?"

Khamiel pulled his boots off and then his pants. "Oh, I've been impressed with you from the very beginning."

She straddled his ankles. Bending at the waist, she lowered her body onto his and slowly slithered up his hard, muscle-toned flesh.

Her lips touched the puckered scar at his knee. She left a trail of kisses as she followed it inch by inch up to his waist.

She moved higher.

The hard length of his shaft slid seductively between her breasts. She paused—and moved lower. Khamiel tilted her chin and when his pink cock peeked through her dark-blue cleavage, she kissed it.

Stan groaned.

With a sassy toss of her hair, she lifted her face, smiled and slowly licked his musk from her lips. "*Mmm*," she purred, "I love the way you taste."

She grasped the edge of his black skin-tight T-shirt and pushed it up over the rippled muscles of his stomach.

He grasped her wrists and pulled. Stan sought her lips in a feverish open-mouth, tongue-probing kiss. As his tongue dueled with hers for dominance, he caressed her back and squeezed the cheeks of her ass.

Khamiel pushed against the mattress with her arms and arched her back giving him access to her breasts.

A further invitation wasn't need.

He cupped and lifted her firm dark-blue flesh. A finger grazed her hardened nipple. Faint red lines shot out across her breast and disappeared. He smiled and rubbed the pad of his finger in a slow circular motion over her nipple. The faint red lines reappeared—pulsating, growing brighter with each revolution.

Stan captured her other nipple between his teeth.

"*Ahh!*" Bright red lines flashed over her breast and like a living, breathing web spread across her chest.

Khamiel swiveled and rocked her hips, grinding her hot flesh against his groin.

He felt the head of his cock penetrate her pussy.

A wild, sensuous grin spread across her face. With a hard, violent downward thrust of her hips, she buried his cock deep inside her.

Almost instantly, the arteries near the surface of her skin became long pulsating pale-pink lines, which grew brighter with each passing moment.

She enveloped him in a cocoon of sensuous warmth.

He gazed into her eyes and fell into their swirling black depths. He knew the words she had asked for, the words she needed to hear.

Stan opened his mouth to blurt it out—*Not now! Don't cheapen this with promises you might not be able to keep.*

Khamiel put her finger against his open lips.

He tore his gaze away from the magnetic pull of her eyes.

Her beautiful body glowed in a deep pulsating blue that spread across the darkened room. Beneath his hands, he felt the growing heat from her red breasts.

Faster and harder, she ground her fevered flesh against him.

He panted for breath—*Wait for her*!

It was one thing to want to wait, but an entirely different matter to do so while her inner muscles milked his cock, stealing his breath and control.

He felt the pressure building. Stan lowered his hands to her waist in an attempt to slow her down, but she jerked his hands back to her breasts.

Stan pulled her to him and rolled across the bed, pinning her against the mattress.

She locked her legs around his hips. "You're not...going—"

He silenced her with a long hard kiss.

"No...we're going...together."

Stan slowed the pace of their lovemaking with long deep thrusts into her hot wet pussy. He ducked his head and captured her nipple between his teeth.

"*Ahh!*" Khamiel grabbed his hair and pulled his face tighter against her breast.

His chest burned, his vision blurred, Stan's fingers clawed at the sheets. His arms stiffened and in a hard flesh pounding thrust, he felt the euphoric release as he climaxed.

Khamiel opened her mouth and gasped. Her back arched off the bed and her fingernails clawed at his back as a reddish-orange hue rippled across her skin like waves of fire.

Stan collapsed, supporting his weight with his elbows, and lay his head upon her heaving breasts.

Her arms encircled his shoulders and she kissed the top of his head. "*Wow*," she whispered.

He chuckled.

"Why did you laugh?"

Stan kissed her breast. "I was thinking it deserved at least two *wows*. Maybe three.

The blue in her skin faded leaving a soft pink breast beneath his cheek. He kissed her again and rolled onto the mattress beside her.

She snuggled closer. "Definitely a three," she mumbled and fell asleep.

The ringing phone pulled Stan from a deep, blissful sleep. He frowned and glanced at the alarm clock on the bedside table. It was three o'clock in the morning.

A few minutes later, there was a soft knock on the door.

He touched the lamp and the bright light momentarily blinded him. "Yeah, Ron. What is it?"

The door opened.

Stan swung his feet from the bed and sat up.

Ron entered, wide-awake and fully dressed. "One of the Navy's amphibious ships has a two hundred ton well-deck door jammed and the Skipper is ready to keelhaul an ensign. Someone got the bright idea that all I have to do is go halfway across the Atlantic and wave a magic wand to fix it."

"Yeah, right," Stan snorted.

"If I find out whose idea it was to call me, the Ensign may have company cleaning barnacles off the ship's hull."

Stan laughed. "Good luck."

With an appreciative glance at Khamiel's nude body sprawled on the bed, Ron gave him a short salute and closed the door.

Stan lifted two fingers to the side of his head returning Ron's good-bye. He turned his upper body at the waist and lowered his gaze. Except for her hair, Khamiel had vanished from view. Her hair rose from the pillow. The mattress shifted as she got out of bed.

"Where are you going?"

"Why, you want to hold my hand while I pee?" She walked into the bathroom. "You could have at least covered me when Ron knocked on the door."

He grimaced. "Sorry."

The door opened and Ron stuck his head back into the room. "One last thing. Try not to break anything while I'm gone."

Chapter Eighteen

In the twilight zone between sleep and fully awake, Stan reached for Khamiel.

Her side of the bed was empty. The sheets were cold.

In the time it took to blink, he rolled from the bed fully awake with his imagination running wild. Had she been so upset over Ron seeing her nude body that she had left him in the early morning hours? Would she go off on her own in search of Wooso? Had Wooso tracked them down and gotten to Khamiel?

Stan snatched his pistol from the nightstand, flipped the safety off and started for the door.

He stopped short, stunned to see a dark-chocolate, sexy woman sunbathing in the nude outside the sliding glass door. Her skin looked rich and creamy. Stan wondered if she tasted as good as she looked...and then quickly chided himself for even thinking about another woman after the night Khamiel had given him.

The woman sat up as Stan opened the door.

"Khamiel!" He stood there with his mouth open.

"Were you expecting someone else?"

"I...ah...no...I didn't recognize you. You're so...so..."

"I was getting some sun." She laughed as her skin lost the dark hue and blended with the light tan covering of the patio recliner. "I think the color was brown."

"I was thinking chocolate." He chuckled. "You have any other colors I don't know about?"

"If I catch you looking at another *woman* like you were looking at me—I might turn a little green around the edges."

"I'll try to remember that."

"You had better." Her arms went around his waist and her warm lips touched his. "Good morning."

"Good morning to you, my little Chameleon." Stan returned the kiss. "How did you sleep?"

She snuggled closer, her breasts pressed against his chest. "I haven't slept that well in a *long* time."

Her low sultry voice stirred the emotions he had felt last night.

"Khamiel," he whispered. "I..." *Go on! Say it.* "I'm going to fix breakfast." *Coward! You big pussy.*

He stepped away from her. "Are you hungry?"

"After last night, I'm starved." She took his hand. "Let's go see what Ron has in the fridge."

Why doesn't he just tell me? I can feel it in the way he touches me and hear it in his voice. What's he scared of?

She knew the answer—commitment...being hurt.

Tell him how you feel.

No! She argued with herself. *I'm not going to force him.*

They walked into the kitchen and she opened the refrigerator door. "Have you thought about our mutual problem?"

He opened a cupboard and found the coffee grounds. "Yes."

Khamiel pulled out some food and closed the door. "Are you going to tell me or do I have to guess?"

Stan filled the coffee pot and turned it on. "I'm going to try and lure her here."

"Here!" She dropped an egg on the floor. "To Ron's house?"

"Sure." He grinned. "Why not here? We place a few sensors around the place and voila! She walks into our trap and it's over."

She squatted down to wipe up the broken egg. "That's the best idea you could come up with?"

"Do you have a better one?" he asked with a smartass grin.

"No." Khamiel wiped the floor dry and stood. "How are you going to lure her here?"

He stared at the coffee pot slowly filling with hot black liquid. "I'm working on it."

"I wouldn't worry much about it. Wooso seems to stay one step ahead of us. She'll probably show up sooner or later on her own."

"That's it!" Stan slammed a fist into an open palm. "Why didn't I think of it?"

He grabbed her head, kissed her cheek and hurried out of the kitchen.

"Think of what? Where are you going?"

"To make a phone call."

Khamiel sighed and turned back to the stove. "I thought he was going to fix breakfast."

The last of the coffee gurgled through. She poured a cup, took a sip and called out, "Coffee's done!"

Stan came into the kitchen with the phone stuck under his chin, picked up *her* cup and gave her a quick kiss on the ear before he went back into the other room.

She watched his receding back. “You’re welcome.”

Two hours later, a delivery truck arrived with several boxes.

Stan looked at Khamiel and winked.

“You’re being awfully secretive about this,” she complained.

“Sorry, I’ve just had a lot on my mind.” He picked up two of the boxes.

The delivery truck had no sooner pulled away, than two telephone repair vans pulled into the drive.

Khamiel stiffened. The workers may have been wearing phone company uniforms, but she recognized each of them. “What is your team doing here?”

“Relax, they’re here to set the surveillance equipment in place and then leave. Course, I had to promise if this didn’t work, we would turn ourselves in.”

“What can I do to help?” she asked.

“For right now.” He paused. “Stay out of the way.”

“Gee, thank you very fucking much.”

“Khamiel!”

She marched through the house, dumped a fresh pot of coffee in the sink and stormed into the bedroom, slamming the door behind her.

She gasped as she viewed the reflection of a very black nude woman in the full-length mirror. “Damn!”

With an exasperated sigh, she flopped onto the bed and concentrated on controlling her anger. Khamiel closed her eyes and began taking long, slow breaths.

A noisy woodpecker woke her up with its insistent pounding on the door. She sat up in bed. How did a woodpecker get into the house?

"Khamiel," Stan's voice replaced the pecking. "May I come in?"

"It's not locked."

The doorknob slowly turned and he inched the door open. "Is it safe?"

"You ever treat me like that again, you might as well go out the front door and don't look back."

"I'm sorry, it's just that if this doesn't go down right—you could get hurt."

She got off the bed and stood by the window. "So could you."

Stan crossed the room to stand behind her. "That's a risk I take every day."

He lifted his arm, held her hair in his hand and let the strands slide through his fingers.

Khamiel leaned back against his broad chest. "Aren't I allowed to make the same choice?"

"No."

"Why not?" she countered just as quickly.

"Because." He sighed. His breath stirred her hair and gently warmed her ear. "It's my job to make sure you're safe."

"Is that the only reason you don't want me involved?"

Stan turned away.

She whirled around. "You can't say it?"

"Say what?"

"If you haven't got the balls to say it," she started past him for the door, "then maybe I'm wasting my time."

He reached out and grabbed hold of her arm. "What the hell are you ranting about?"

"Damn you, Stanley Freeman." She turned to face him. "Do you love me or not? Now's the time to say so, because I need to know just where I stand."

"Why now?" he whispered.

"Because, if you are doing this simply as your duty, then I'm out of here and out of your life. You'll never have to baby-sit me again."

Stan frowned as if in agony. "And if I'm doing this because I love you?"

"Then we're going to do this together, because you're not facing that *bitch* alone."

She waited for what seemed an eternity. Her heart felt like it was pounding in her throat.

"I—" He lifted his hand and touched her hair. As the silky strands flowed through his fingers, his eyes filled with longing. "With all my heart, I love you."

Khamiel jumped into his arms. "Took you long enough to say it."

Their lips met in a long tender kiss.

She swung her feet back to the ground. "Now, my dear, show me what you have planned for our uninvited guest."

Chapter Nineteen

Khamiel paced the floor.

Everything was set. Stan had made the prearranged radio transmission giving away their location. Half of his team had the place under electronic surveillance. Anything that moved toward or away from Ron's house would be seen instantly. If he was right, and Wooso was monitoring their normal operating frequency, it wouldn't be long before she arrived. If not, they were going to be in for a very long night and come morning, Stan would be forced to surrender to his men.

Khamiel didn't like waiting with nothing to do. With each hour that passed, her hatred of Wooso grew for killing her mother and turning her own life upside down. Right now, she hated Stan for the very things that caused her heart to beat faster when he was near.

On the other side of the room, the glow from three laptop computers bathed his face in soft pastel shades of ever changing light. His eyes never stopped moving between the screens as he monitored the hidden cameras, motion sensors and microphones surrounding Ron's house. He looked confident and strong, even though they were soon to face a very formidable foe.

A bead of sweat rolled down his neck.

Khamiel looked out the thick plate glass window. Mother Nature had come to Gainesville and she was pissed. Heavy clouds obscured the moon and stars. The wind howled, whipping the trees into a frenzy of continuous motion. Lightening flashed across the sky and for a brief moment, she saw Ron's cabin cruiser, the *Belleau Wood's Baby,* straining at her mooring lines as the white-capped waves slammed into its hull.

The night was perfect—for *Han Shi.* The one the Chinese called, Black Death.

The headset Stan had given her crackled. "Viper, we have movement on the face of the cliff...about halfway up, but the infrared signature is too small to be a person."

Khamiel ran across the room and searched one of the screens. "I don't see anything."

Stan held up his hand to silence her. As he studied the screen, he keyed his microphone. "Was contact consistent with the reading of an MAC Suit?"

"What's a MAC Suit?" Khamiel asked.

"Viper! That's classified!"

She wasn't sure who was on the headset, but by the tone of his voice—he was pissed.

Stan turned off the voice activated transmit key and kept his eyes glued to the screen.

"MAC," he explained, "or Malarse Cryogenic Suit, as it is officially named, is a lightweight micro-conductive material used to reduce human heat signatures from infrared detection," his shoulders slumped as he sighed, "and *was* highly classified."

"Viper...suspicions confirmed. Target signature consistent with MAC test signatures."

Stan keyed the transmit button. “Copy.”

He looked up from the computer screens. “There’s still time to leave. Are you sure you want to go through with this?”

Khamiel softly touched his cheek. “Are you walking away?”

She saw the answer in the determined set of his jaw.

“Even if I could, I wouldn’t,” he said stoically

“For better or worse.” She leaned over and kissed him on the lips. “I’m staying.”

“Khamiel, I—”

She put her finger across his lips. “Tell me later.” A tripped sensor near the edge of the cliff flashed on the screen. “We have company.”

Stan stood. “Remember what I told you. The Chinese call her *Black Death* for a reason. You get the chance—take her out. Don’t hesitate. Don’t think about it. Just do it.”

He reached toward her, found her chin and tilted her head up. “There’s one more thing.”

“I know, don’t get between the two of you.”

“Besides that.” He lowered his head and took her lips in a hard, demanding kiss.

The kiss stopped as suddenly as it started. “Take a couple deep breaths. You’re turning blue.”

Khamiel got her racing heart under control. “I thought you liked *blue*?”

Another light began flashing on the screen.

“She’s at the back door.”

His voice sounded calm, but she detected a faint nervous quivering in his vocal cords. She felt his increased heart rate and blood flow beneath his skin. Was he remembering his last confrontation with Wooso, the Chinese *Han Shi?*

Stan gave her hand a squeeze and moved across the room to take his position at the top of the stairs.

Khamiel padded across the floor. She picked up a silenced .222 caliber, M-19 sniper rifle and opened the sliding glass door. Dropping to the floor, she crawled to the edge of the balcony. Her Chameleon eyes took in the roof of the lower section of the house and the yard in a single glance.

Other than the wind blown trees—nothing moved.

She heard the faint comforting sound of Stan's shallow breathing in her headset.

Aim and squeeze the trigger. Just like at the range. I can do this, she kept telling herself, but deep down, she wasn't sure. In her short time at the FBI, she had only fired a weapon at one other person—and missed.

Her mind raced, torn with conflicting emotion. She envisioned Janice lying on her kitchen table with Stan's knife stuck in her heart...Stan's bullet scarred body...and her mother lying in an open coffin.

"You bet your sweet and sour, North Korea loving, Chinese ass I can do this," she breathed aloud.

Stan chuckled. "Having doubts?"

Khamiel flipped the safety off her weapon. "Not any more," she whispered into the microphone.

Movement at the far edge of the lower roof caught her attention and she focused on it. Fingers clutching the edge quickly changed into a crouching person dressed in dull black from head to toe.

She lifted the rifle to her shoulder. "Shit! She's wearing night-goggles."

Khamiel squeezed the trigger. *Pufffft.* The rifle butt slammed into her shoulder.

The impact lifted the crouching figure off the roof. She clutched her chest and disappeared from view.

"She's down!" Khamiel panted into her microphone as adrenaline kicked her heart into overdrive. "I got her! She's down!"

"Do you see a body?"

"I got her in the chest. I saw the impact."

"Khamiel! Do you *see* the body?"

"No, she went off the roof, but the impact knocked her night-vision goggles off. They're still on the roof."

"Your dead body just tripped another sensor."

She stared at the rifle in her hands and then at the goggles lying on the roof. Her mind played back the impact of the bullet in slow motion. Something was missing...but what? What wasn't she seeing?"

Blood. Damn it, there was no blood.

"That's impossible!"

"Not if she's wearing a Kevlex suit."

"What's that? Another classified toy."

"Unfortunately," Stan exhaled on a long tired sigh. "Kevlex is the latest in Nano-technology. It's as bullet proof as Kevlar, fire retardant as Nomex and fits the body like a spandex glove."

Her fingers tightened around the stock of the M-17 and turned black.

"Is there anything that you know for certain that she hasn't stolen?" she hissed through her gritted teeth.

"Yeah—you."

"That's a comforting thought."

"Here's another. If you hit her in the chest, she's hurt. Probably a broken rib, maybe two."

"Whoopee," she whispered in a fit of sarcastic frustration.

She concentrated her thoughts on her breathing and away from her anger. Her fingers slowly disappeared, blending into the rich teak wood of the stock.

"She knows my location." Khamiel gathered her feet under her and sprinted for the far end of the balcony. "I'm moving."

Khamiel reached the railing and flung herself to the floor as an arrow screamed past her head.

The sound of glass breaking on the first floor reached her ears. She looked over the side to see a pair of legs going through the window.

"She's inside," Khamiel whispered.

"Take cover."

The night erupted in a blaze of orange flame and white smoke as the building shook beneath her. Windows in the first floor of Ron's house shattered, filling the air with shards of deadly razor sharp glass. A second explosion followed three seconds later.

"I'm going in."

"Stan! Wait!"

The sound of automatic weapons fire erupted in the room below her. Normally, she would never have attempted the jump. *Go ahead, you can do it. Trust the Chameleon.*

Her mind calculated the exact distance to the ground as she leapt over the railing. Dropping almost twenty feet, she landed in a crouch and dove through a blown out window.

She was just in time to see Stan take a wicked right kick to the head and another to his left hip. With a heavy grunt, Stan folded, bounced off the wall and landed in an unmoving heap. The bitter iron odor of fresh blood mixed with cordite bit at the lining of her nose.

"So nice of you to drop in, Khamiel. It saves me the trouble of finding you."

She saw Wooso's arm muscles tighten and the flick of her wrist. Khamiel turned sideways and let the jagged flying disk pass by.

"Not bad." Wooso reached inside a loose fold of her black garment. As she pulled her hand out, her wrist snapped forward like a striking rattlesnake.

Khamiel saw two spinning disks cutting through the air. She ducked and spun away as they stuck in the wall where she had been standing.

Fire clawed its way across her arm and face as a third and forth disk found their marks.

"I can keep this up all day," Wooso gloated. "As long as you are breathing and sweating, I'll know where you are. Why don't you give up quietly? I'll even spare Stan's life."

Khamiel wiped the blood from her face. "Fuck you."

"You want to fucky me?" Wooso laughed. "What's the matter?" she taunted in an exaggerated heavy accent. "Stan lost his touch and can't satisfy you."

Khamiel slowed her breathing and concentrated on cooling her skin all the while never taking her eyes off of her antagonist. She studied her. The way she held her fingers, the muscles in her arms and legs. Her eyes focused on each tiny detail and her mind memorized them.

The next movement was a blur, impossible to see with the human eye, but hers were far from normal.

Khamiel turned to the side, arched her back and reached behind her. As her fingers closed around a shiny, spinning wheel of death, she pivoted and sent it flying back across the room.

Kevlar had one bad flaw—it wouldn't stop a knife. She was counting on the new Kevlex to have the same flaw.

Wooso moved to the right...into the path of the five-pointed star. Her hand went to her left breast.

Khamiel saw the shock and surprise in her eyes as her hand came away covered in blood.

"You mutant *bitch*!" Wooso screamed as she launched herself across the room.

Khamiel smiled.

She ducked under a flying leg kick, grabbed the ankle and shoved up with all her strength.

Wooso's back slammed into the wall and she landed with a heavy *thud* on the floor. She got up slowly, but not with empty hands.

In her right hand, she held a butterfly knife. With one shake of her wrist, the thin blade lay open. Wrapped around her other hand, Wooso held a long silver chain. On the end of it dangled a wicked looking spiral of sharpened steel.

"I'm going to fillet you like a fish."

"You've tried that already *Han Shi*." She ran her fingers across her cheek and smiled. "How come you're the only one bleeding around here?"

"But, I—I cut you."

She saw the woman's self-confidence waver.

"It was such a tiny little scratch," Khamiel taunted. "I can't even feel it anymore."

The end of the chain started bouncing. With a flick of her wrist, Wooso sent the spinning dart straight for her heart.

She batted it aside and felt the twisted blades shred the skin on the back of her hand.

Wooso's eyes gleamed in sadistic pleasure. "*Tsk, tsk, tsk,* Khamiel, that wasn't very smart. Which hand did I get? You do that again, it will look like ground meat."

The two stepped over the blast debris as they slowly circled.

Wooso faked with the chain and lunged with the knife.

Khamiel easily avoided both.

A flying foot caught her in the stomach. She let the force of the blow carry her away from the danger.

"I'm going to win," Wooso taunted. "Why don't you just give in and admit defeat. It'll save you *soooo* much pain."

Khamiel moved closer. "You have to cut me first."

Wooso smirked. "Oh, I think I got you good that time."

Khamiel flexed her fingers. She held her hand up like she was checking her nails. "Gee, I guess you did at that."

The last of the wound sealed shut. She turned her hand around. "It was so small I almost didn't even see it."

Wooso looked down at the blood-covered steel.

Khamiel drew back and let a right hook fly. She felt bone shatter beneath her fist. The impact jarred her arm clear back to her shoulder.

The feared *Han Shi,* the dreaded Black Death, went down on one knee.

As she started to get up, Khamiel followed through with a flying kick to the back of her head.

Wooso toppled forward. She lay sprawled, unmoving on the floor.

Khamiel, wary of any tricks, crept closer and slowly turned her over. The handles of the butterfly knife lay open on her foe's chest, with the blade buried between her breasts.

Stan limped over to stand beside her. "Looks like I missed one hell of a fight."

"Stanley." Blood gurgled from Wooso's lips. She lifted her hand to her neck and pulled a thin gold chain from under her Kevlex suit. With her last ounce of strength, Wooso broke the chain.

Her bloody fingers opened.

Khamiel knelt and took a small gold ring from the palm of her hand. "I take it—this was yours."

She saw a lone tear slip from the corner of Stan's eye. It hung suspended on his cheek, refusing to fall.

Stan turned and limped away.

Chapter Twenty

Black shadows dove through the windows and doors.

Red laser dots crisscrossed the room and came to rest on the body of Wooso.

"Sorry to disappoint you, but she's dead." Khamiel shook her head in disgust. "Nice of y'all to finally show up."

One by one, the red dots blinked off and flashlights came on.

"Viper, are you injured?" Chelae asked.

"It's nothing." Stan started up the stairs to the second floor. "Secure the area, Viper One and see what you can do about getting the lights back on in here."

"Yes, sir."

Chelae picked up Wooso's chain and examined the deadly tips. "Khamiel, do you need medical attention?"

"I'm fine."

"These blades are covered in blood." She held the end of the chain under the glare of her flashlight. "Is it yours?"

"Yes, but it's just a scratch."

Chelae chuckled. "I guess I'll have to take your word for it."

"Thank you. Now if you don't need me for anything, I'm going to check on Stan. He took a hard blow to the head and was unconscious for several minutes."

"He was knocked out?" Alarm filled her voice. "Doc, check Viper for possible concussion."

The team's paramedic ran up the stairs.

"Chelae, why didn't you tell me *she* was Stan's wife?"

Chelae looked away. "You know?"

Khamiel opened her hand and showed her the ring. "She tried to give this to Stan before she died."

"It's not something we discuss among team members." Chelae's shoulders slumped. "But I'm glad for his sake that it was you who took her out."

"Did he…love her?"

"At one time his world revolved around her…until he found out her true identity." Chelae knelt down and examined Wooso's clothing. "It appears Stan wasn't the only one under her influence. She's wearing one of our experimental MAC suits and Kevlex."

"Stan suspected as much."

Chelae's head came up. Her eyebrows narrowed.

Khamiel grinned. "He told me about them."

"Under the circumstances," Chelae stood, "I guess you had a need to know what you were facing."

"Would someone get this piece of shit out of here," she ordered. "Where the hell are the lights?"

"May I go now?" Khamiel asked.

"Yeah, go on. While you're at it, pour yourself a stiff drink." Chelae smiled. "You earned it."

Khamiel reached the top of the stairs and passed a dour-faced, grumbling paramedic. “Damn pig-headed...should've hit him harder. Oh, sorry, Khamiel...ah...maybe you can talk some sense into him. He won't let me examine him.”

“What's the matter?” she asked.

“He said if didn't get my flashlight out of his face, I'd have to bend over and walk backwards to use it.”

“Then you better make yourself scarce. I'll see what I can do.” As she walked toward the stairs, she shook her head and muttered. “Wonder if I should use Ron's fry pan.”

Stan sat at the desk with his shirt off and a bloody bandage around his arm. He hung up the phone as she approached. “Did she send you up here too?”

Khamiel shook her head. “No! She didn't.” She reached out to examine his injury. “What the hell is this?”

“It's nothing. Just a scratch.”

“You call a gunshot wound a scratch?” she fumed.

“Depends on where you get shot,” he said with a smile.

“Why were you so rough on your medic? He's just doing his job.”

“Doc was being a pain-in-the-ass. I was making a report to the office and he kept shining that damn flashlight in my eyes.”

“The medic was right, she should have hit you harder.”

He got up from the chair and went to the wet bar. “He said that?” Stan laughed as he poured a double whiskey.

“You want one?”

She crossed the floor and took his glass. “Thanks.”

Khamiel went outside and leaned on the railing. Her hand shook as she lifted her glass and emptied it.

Stan took the glass from her. "First time is always the hardest."

"Does it ever get any easier?" Her voice trembled as she took his glass and drained it.

"No, and I hope it never does." He put his arm around her waist. "I think that's what separates us and *them.* You take people like Wooso, the terrorist—and the serial killers down through history—they don't have a conscience. They kill for the thrill, the perverted power they feel at taking another's life."

She opened her other hand. "This is yours."

He looked at the ring for several long moments. Then with a long sigh, Stan took the wedding band, stepped to the side and flung it as far as he could out into the night.

"It won't do much to remove the bad memories, but it closes the book on a bad chapter of my life."

Khamiel stepped into his arms. "Then maybe it's time to open a new book."

"As long as you're there to help me fill it with new memories."

She lifted her head and met his lips in a kiss that was sure to fill their first page together. "I thought you'd never ask."

Khamiel stood in the middle of the room and surveyed the damage under the daylight. "What are we going to do about this?"

Stan gave her shoulder a light squeeze. "Don't worry about it. There's a clean up crew on the way. They should be here by tomorrow. By the time they leave, Ron won't even know we were here."

"Suppose, just for a moment, that Ron gets home before they finish."

A smirk lifted the corner of his mouth. "I was assured that wouldn't happen."

"And your source of information came from high up the chain-of-command?"

He wiggled his eyebrows. "The very highest."

"What's she like—in person?" Khamiel snuggled inside the circle of his arms.

"I'll let you decide that for yourself," he whispered in her hair.

"What do you mean?" She turned her head and looked up into his face.

"We've been invited to the White House."

"Really!" she squealed in excitement. "Wow! When do we go?"

"I have to check with her secretary who will have to check with the Chief of Staff who will—"

"Alright," she laughed, "I get the picture."

Stan's arms tightened around her, "The president wanted to me to tell you that the doctors at the lab aren't going to quit searching for a way to reverse the Chameleon formula."

"That's great."

She grew quiet as she contemplated the news. Life had been so predictable before with her small apartment, a nine to five job with good pay and...so damn boring. Khamiel looked around the room. It felt damn good to know that she had taken out the *Han Shi*. What could an FBI lab give her to compensate for the adrenaline rush of this? *Nothing!*

"What happens," she whispered, "until then? What am I going to do?"

"Come work with the team. I'm sure we can find some way to use your new abilities."

"I think…I'd like that."

Stan smiled. "I was hoping you would and so was the president."

"Wow, imagine that, I'm actually going to the White House."

"We might get to go twice." Stan laughed softly in her ear. "Maybe even spend the night."

"You're kidding, right?"

"The president has offered the use of her Rose Garden." He lowered his head and kissed her cheek. "How about it? Think you'd like to be married in the Rose Garden and spend our honeymoon night in the Lincoln Room."

"Yes, my love." Khamiel turned in his arms and kissed him. "It sounds wonderful, but there's just one problem…I don't have anything to wear."

Stan laughed. "I don't think anyone will notice."

She stepped out of his arms.

"Where are you going?"

"I thought we might celebrate."

He followed her up the stairs.

Khamiel found a bottle of champagne and popped the plastic top.

Stan lifted his eyebrows. "Isn't it a little early in the day for that?"

She handed him a long stemmed glass. "This occasion calls for a toast." Khamiel lifted her glass. "To the Rose Garden."

He shook his head. "No, to us."

Khamiel closed her eyes, smiled and kissed Stan's lips. "To us."

About the Author

To learn more about R Casteel, please visit www.rcasteel.net. Send an email to rcasteel@rcasteel.net.

Look for these titles

Coming Soon:

Texas Thunder by R. Casteel

Sex can be the most devastating weapon

Scorch

© 2007 Nage Archer

Frank Aston has what most men would consider a dream job. As bodyguard to Lady Jacqueline, the heir to Baron Ceston's throne and fortune, he gets to watch her every moment of every day. He knows each inch of her cruel, tantalizing body from her almost black eyes to her long, sensuous legs. But he can never lay a hand on her, not even to save his own life. He can't even reveal a conspiracy against his own liege, the baron, for fear some harm will come to her. On the other hand, Lady Jacqueline has absolutely no regard for his safety or sanity at all.

Lady Jacqueline's dangerous string of seductions leads Frank deeper and deeper into a conspiracy he's unable to reveal. Worse still, the heiress is hell bent on dominating him, breaking his will until he becomes just another man willing to do anything to please his Mistress.

Available now in ebook from Samhain Publishing.

Printed in the United Kingdom
by Lightning Source UK Ltd.
121731UK00001B/68/A

9 781599 984155